HOW TO KILL A SUPERHERO

A GAY BONDAGE MANUAL

PABLO GREENE

FIRST EDITION

Designed by Nick Agin

ISBN-10: 0615896820
ISBN-13: 978-0615896823

To my superfriend M.

CONTENTS

INTRODUCTION

If you have ever thought that a superhero would make a perfect character for a pornographic book, you're not alone. Superheroes' muscular bodies and virtuous heroics shape many dreams. When I was entering adolescence, the stories of superheroes sparked an interest in bondage and domination in me that I could not explain. When these superheroes are caught by a villain — and let's not forget how often they end up bound and gagged as a result — strong sexual fires open up.

The novel you hold in your hands contains strong graphical elements of BDSM and fetish. In these pages you will find references to bondage, sadism, masochism, spanking, domination, breath control, water sports, sexual slavery and power exchange. This story also contains graphic references to sexual fetishes, such as sports uniforms, lycra and spandex, suits, rubber, feet, sweat and urine, boots and of course, men in superhero uniforms. It is a work of fiction.

The domination and bondage themes in this book are meant for adults, and I strongly encourage you to read books like *The New Bottoming Book, The New Topping Book* by Dossie Eaton or Jay Wiseman's *SM 101* to learn about healthy approaches to incorporating BDSM into your sexuality and personal health. Connecting with kink and BDSM communities may also provide you with new perspectives that can allow to have fun but also stay safe. This book would not be possible without the support of members of these communities.

I hope you enjoy Roland's story.

Pablo Greene
New Orleans, Louisiana

CHAPTER 1
MY SUPERHERO FETISH

My name is Roland.

On the night of my 28th birthday, my friends took me out for dinner. We shared heaps of enchiladas, frosty bottles of beer, limes on the rim. I tossed back a couple of shots. I blew out candles on a red velvet cake, and our waitress led all of us at the table in an off-key rendition of the happy birthday song. Earlier, I had left my car at home on purpose, because I knew I would have a beer or two at the restaurant. By the time we paid the bill, I had drunk seven bottles and downed four shots. I walked home from dinner alone, comforted by the false safety provided by my cell phone and the gauzy softness of my whiskey buzz.

It was only midnight, but my neighborhood was a quiet one at this hour. As I walked, I heard nothing more than my own steps as they hit the sidewalk. As I turned the corner onto my street, a person jumped on me from behind. Quick jabs to my kidneys brought me down to my knees, and something sharp punctured my skin. The attacker used that sharp object, once, twice, and up to 24 times. He stabbed me squarely between the shoulder blades, coming very close to my spine, slicing through my muscle tissue like a butcher and missing my neck by just an inch. I lay bleeding on the street until a car full of teenagers happened to find me. They called 911.

When the ambulance brought me in, the blood loss and the shock from the attack sent me into cardiac arrest. I blacked out.

The medics on duty later said that my blackout lasted nothing more than a few seconds, but during that time, I floated in the plane between life and death. At first I only floated in a pool of darkness and silence. But after a few moments, I caught a gleam, a pinpoint of white and gold light in the distance. You could call it a vision, I guess. I don't have a name for it.

The light cut through that dark blanket of severe physical trauma, and I saw symbols fly in front of me, like fireworks from another planet with its own laws of physics. These floating symbols did not represent God, I don't think. I can't be sure. They flew past me like celestial bodies in the cosmos.

I heard no voices, and there was no sense of "moving toward the light." As the white and gold shapes orbited around me, they grew, until they exploded into a mass of light. It shot out like a bolt of lightning and filled my chest with something that felt cold and hot at the same time. Something that burned. A buzzing sound cut through the silence. My ears rang. I regained consciousness soon after.

It took the doctors hours and several pints of blood to close my wounds and bring me back to a stable condition. I awoke two days later. The wounds went deep into my tissues, but my vital organs and main arteries had been spared. I was lucky.

My recovery came next. I was a shitty patient. Every minute I spent in the intensive care unit, every moment laid up in that bed, I wanted to get up, and go back to my job.

I remained in the hospital for a week, and I went back to work just six days after I was sent home. I was head nurse at Arkum Memorial Hospital, and the team needed me back at work. I filled my schedule in our computer system to take as many shifts as I could for that month of June. I loved my job.

I didn't spend much time thinking back to the blackout and the golden fireworks I had witnessed the night of my stabbing. I was a man of science, and I attributed the visions I saw on the night of my attack to disturbances in my optic nerve, as well as the probable lack of oxygen as my body fought off death. In nursing school I learned that the pineal gland in the brain can often trigger visions of near-death experiences during major traumas, like mine. This gland will trigger the release of compounds that will make a person see images, lights, and other visions. I suspect that my pineal gland might have gone out of whack the night of my attack, though I am not exactly sure how.

I never found out who the mugger was. The attacker stole my credit cards, and exactly 38 dollars in cash.

I suppose I could say that I might have been scared to go back out in the world at night again, for fear of another mugging, but the truth was, I wanted to prove to myself that what had happened to me was random, without any meaning. And I was damned if an incident like this was going to keep me imprisoned in my own apartment.

In the weeks that followed, I resolved to live the life I wanted, to squeeze the most of out of every moment. The way to do this was to try things that I had previously been too scared to do.

This resolve reminded me of how much I had yet to live. I was missing something real, something to hold onto, and I knew that I was never going to find it by staying home along after my recovery was complete.

On the three-week anniversary of my stabbing, I went out by myself. This was something I never would have done before. I took a taxi to Fortress in the warehouse district. Fortress was a large nightclub that promised dark corners, sweaty bodies, and the seduction of anonymity. I went there to find someone to take home.

I would give it my best shot, and if I was successful, I may find a way to get laid, and put the past behind me. I needed sex to find release, and though I was too shy to admit it to my friends, I knew I could admit it to myself: I needed a good, deep fucking.

I hadn't had sex in more than two years, and I felt hollow, dried out like a scarecrow.

Nothing was going to let me feel this emptiness again. I headed into the cavernous warehouse of Fortress that night, feeling unsure of my ability to attract any men, yet I was certain that I was looking for something.

That night I found *him*.

◆

He told me his name was Rick, and that he had a superhero fetish.

His eyes were green and his hair fell in waves, brushing the nape of his neck. The muscles of his chest were bursting through his t-shirt. He stood a good eight inches taller than me, and his muscular shoulders cast a shadow as he leaned in toward the mass of people dancing. The sound system exploded with music, and the bodies dancing around us steamed up the place with heat. House and techno had never sounded better to me.

We had met by touching first. Our backs bumped into each other, and I spilled my beer. I turned and faced a man packed with muscle, his chest tapering down to a small waist and supported by muscular legs. His biceps bulged out of his short sleeves. I smiled up at him, unsure of what was the best way to respond. He smiled, but only partially. He inspected me while he danced.

"Hey, what's your name?" he said. "I'm Rick."

In my mind, in my perverted, twisted little mind, where big muscle jocks became superheroes, I knew that a man like this one could fill out a superhero's tights without a problem.

It was fucking unreal.

He was fucking unreal.

Guys this good-looking didn't generally make out with guys like me. They usually walked right past. Those guys always wanted muscle men, and I would never be a muscle man.

I looked for Rick's boyfriend or a posse of friends. He moved with ease, swaying his hips, focused on nothing except the music. He seemed to be alone here tonight, like me.

"So you're into superheroes, huh?" he said.

My heart sank in fear, and just as it plunged, excitement rose inside me in the opposite direction.

The t-shirt I was wearing had to be the telltale sign, and I knew it. Before I left my apartment, I had yanked the blue tee over my head, thinking, why not wear this for a night out? Its shape was nothing but gorgeous geometry: a diamond stretched inside another diamond. This was the logo of The Fighter, one of my favorite superhero icons.

Let's be real. Only comic book dorks or gay guys would wear a shirt like this one. I took a chance, and the shirt was the very thing that started our conversation.

I secretly fantasized about superheroes and the sex they might have with each other.

Rick traced the outline of the diamond logo, and I felt electric shocks where his index finger touched me through the fabric. I imagined that he could visualize what was inside my mind, how much that fantasy made me hard, how it made me feel like fire in my chest, in my throat, and between my legs and in my balls. I hoped my Fighter t-shirt enhanced my narrow chest enough to keep Rick interested.

He smiled at me, tugging at the loops in my belt to jam me closer to him. My own two pecs bumped up against the hard mounds of muscle of his chest. "I work in advertising!" he shouted. "Nursing!" I responded.

I have often felt that time passes at a different pace when dancing in a nightclub. Sometimes, memories flash back like the strobe lights that explode above. They show up, and then they are gone again. I put my hand on Rick's waist, and one of these strobe light memories exploded onto me.

I was back in nursing school, in California, studying in a library carrel. I was reading an organic chemistry book, with my head down. I was wearing a Fighter t-shirt. I was studying to become a nurse because all my life I have wanted to help people, the way that my favorite superheroes from comic books helped those who needed it most. In order to become the best at what I did, I mastered knowledge: the systems of the body, its diseases and its strengths. School suited me, and I spent many years in university and nursing school, surrounded by the questions about the body: How do bodies work, and why do they grow? Why does disease strike? And how do we die? These questions had started every time I had flipped through the stories of The Fighter, The Overfiend, or their arch enemies, like The Dark Matter, Aracniss, or Black Flag. In that library carrel, I saved my comics for the end of the night, as a treat after my studies.

The nightclub popped back into my view. I put my face close to Rick's collarbone, my nose and lips just a couple of inches from his neck. Rick wore no cologne, but his skin tasted like ocean. He shouted over the music, but I shook my head. I put my hand up to my ear. *Can't hear you.*

"Can't hear you," I shouted.

He repeated himself. "You heard me right," he said. "I fucking love superheroes."

His voice rang deep, cutting through the noise of the bass, and I felt myself harden under my jeans.

I knew there were other guys like me, guys who felt a little perverted jerking off on images from their comic book memories, but as far as I knew I had never met any of them in real life. The chances of finding someone who could fall deep into fantasies about superhumans, was slim to none, as far as I was concerned.

On the Internet, it was a whole different story, though. Online, there were hundreds of men who shared my fetish, and I chatted with them many times. But not once in my life did I ever seriously consider meeting them in person. Too many weirdos, too many creeps. Too many serial killers.

Rick let go of my waist, and he put his beefy arm around me. The dark hairs on the forearm ran in the same direction. Orderly, neat, and extremely enticing. I thought he could be Latin American or from an Arab country. Maybe Italy. He walked me to the edge of the dance floor, toward the bar. He bought me a beer, and he asked me to tell him my story. His green eyes glinted under the lights. Then they went back to their opaque state.

"My story, huh?" I said. I laughed a little. I explained where I worked, and why I loved Kansas City. I explained why I came back from California to live in my hometown after graduation, and as he turned sideways in mid-dance, I got a look at the perfect curve of his bubble ass and the way clothes clung to his tight body. He looked healthy and strong, and I wanted to be naked next to him, to feel how my own smaller, shorter self would measure up against his knees, his thighs, his back, and his shoulder blades. I took a swig from my beer, and another strobe-light memory burst in my mind.

I was a kid again, ten years old, and my hair was so blond it was almost white. It was Friday afternoon after school, and I ran home with a pile of the latest issues of my favorite superhero comics and read them in the far corner of my bedroom, my body submerged in a bean bag. I traced the muscles of all my favorite superheroes with my fingers, and after I finished reading my stack, I traced them on white paper with a pencil. I liked neatness and order in everything I did. On my desk in my bedroom, I placed neat stacks of my favorite comics, and in the drawer beneath, the drawings I made of their sculpted bodies. I drew The Fighter, his brother Centaur, and their double-crossing teammate, The Overfiend. I tied a towel around my neck and ran down the length of the house, leaping as I burst onto the backyard. "Long live The Fighter," I screamed.

The crash of electronic rumbles and synthesizer brought me back to the glass bar I was leaning against. Rick glanced at some other guys as they walked nearby, and he inspected their bodies, too. He looked experienced at finding what he wanted in a place like this. In profile, his Roman nose gave his face a hard look, like an eagle in profile. He was physically fit beyond belief, and out of my league by far. I imagined what he might look like in a pair of tights and a bodysuit delineating the muscled lines of his chest. He looked out at the hundreds of men before us, as if we might be watching the waves of the ocean crash. With his left hand he took hold of my ass and gave it a squeeze. He caught me off guard, and I jumped. I turned up to look at him, and before I could say anything he gave me a quick kiss on the lips.

I saw the strobe-light memories dance in my mind again.

I was sixteen years old, and it was summer. My parents' divorce was finally real, and movers were taking out my father's stuff in big boxes. I stood on the porch, watching three thick men carry out my father's belongings, when I caught a burst of colors sticking out from the trash bins in front of our house. I lifted the lid and saw seven boxes, stuffed to the brim with my comic book collection. Other discarded liquids had fallen on top of the comics, ruining them. Their pulp clumped together as they absorbed the liquid. Either my father or my mother had thrown them out, moving me out of a phase of my childhood against my will. The face of The Fighter peered up at me from the wet pages of his comic. I took this last comic and walked behind our house. There, I jerked off to the pages where the Fighter lay bound to a train track with steel chains, his mouth gagged, and his muscles bulging through his costume. I came in thick spurts onto the pages of that comic, and I yanked my cock back into my boxer shorts when I heard one of the movers come out through the side door. I zipped up my jeans and I went back to the dumpster.

I grabbed as many of the comics as I could, and I walked down to the park at the end of our street. I lit a match to my comics and saw them go up in black smoke that made my eyes water and my throat choke. It wasn't the last time I would ever own comic books, but that day I wanted them gone forever.

A trickle of heat brought me back to the dance floor. Rick pressed his other hand onto the spot of skin above my belt, where the edge of my t-shirt gave him access to my bare torso. His hand pressed down firmly, and I blushed. Everyone could see him feel me up under my shirt. Everyone.

"Some of my favorite storylines come from Titan comics," Rick said. "If it weren't for The Fighter's travel to the Ultraworld, the whole imprint would have gone to shit. But it didn't. I have all issues starting from number 137."

"Wow," I said. "I stopped collecting them in high school, but I sometimes look at an issue or two. I just can't believe you get off on them the way I do."

"There's nothing hotter," Rick said. He gave my bulge a hard tug that sent a delicious bolt of pain through me.

We didn't last long inside the club. Rick took my hand and led me out through the stairway, onto the side entrance. I could see the dense muscles on his shoulders churn under his shirt and his muscular ass stride with power under his tight jeans. We walked past some really hot guys, all of them looking for sex, and all of them hotter, bigger and more physically impressive than me. But I was the one whose hand Rick was holding. I was his, and he was mine. For a few brief moments, I didn't feel like a nerd.

I had been single for years, and since then, I had figured out that I was better off alone, free of a relationship. I woke up each morning eager to perform my duties at the hospital, and at night, I slept deeply, and without dreams. This freedom left me with a lot of time to dedicate to my work, and that kept me happy. The only thing I was missing in my life was the fire of good sex, the taste of a man's body on my lips, and the thick mass of a cock inside me.

I fantasized about finding a satisfying sex life during my walks in the prairies outside the suburbs, or in my walks in Powell Gardens, but I always put the fantasies away by the time I was home, in what I called the real world.

I used to call that Kansas City and its buildings, its objects — my apartment, clothes, my books, my triathlon bike, my photographs of my friends and family — the real world.

That had been back then. After the night I met Rick, things became different.

Outside Fortress, the fantasy veneer of the club vanished. The laser and techno landscape was gone, and there was no glamor left. Glamor was stupid. These streets were still considered the rough part of town, and it wasn't wise to hang about at this hour of night. Poverty and racial inequality were real here. My own reality was apparent to me, too.

I stood in the street now, in my bargain jeans from a big box store, and my eyes bathed in orange light from the streetlamps. But Rick didn't care about my clothes. He pushed me up against his parked car, and his long hair and his aftershave filled my nose and eyes.

He drove a silver Audi. I thought it was sort of ridiculous in a mid-life-crisis kind of way, but there's no way he was middle aged. I guessed that at most he was 32, with the intense gaze of a mature man but the muscular body of a college athlete.

"Why don't you come back to my place?" I offered. I lived alone, and I wasn't going to pass up this opportunity. I wanted him in my bed, and I wanted him now.

"We're fine out here," he said. "For now. Maybe afterward." Rick's words gave out firm commands, and this tone of voice he used made me alert, aroused, and eager to hear him talk again.

He put his hands on his fly.

When he unbuttoned his jeans, I felt a surge in my crotch, a blast of heat. I was hard under my Levi's, and I kissed his long neck, running my lips over his stiff stubble, and he smiled down at me with his green eyes. I had never done something like this. How many times had I gone out to a bar with my buddies, only to be left behind nursing a gin and tonic while they took off with the men of their dreams?

Too many times. But I was the guy no one ever noticed. I was the guy that was too plain, too ordinary to take a guy home. I was the guy who always left the bar alone at the end of the night.

Except now, here I was, and the wind was rippling Rick's blue shirt, and I could see it part in the middle, revealing a rock-hard stomach covered in a narrow trail of smooth black hairs. The skin was tan and taut. When I glanced back up at his gorgeous face, I realized that the ethnicities he could fall under had expanded. He could be Mexican, Italian, maybe Turkish. And maybe, he was as American as hamburgers and hot dogs. It was hard to say.

I felt the small of his back, and his packed muscles shifted. The boulders of his ass felt heavy and warm under the palms of my hands. I was breathing hard, trying to keep up with his kisses. To be honest, I had never put my arms around a man that was this muscular. I felt awkward holding this dense mass, as if I were hugging a refrigerator.

"So, about that superhero stuff," I said. "Were you serious? Or did you only say it in order to get into my pants?"

Rick ignored me and kissed me harder. I kissed back.

The tip of my dick was throbbing, and I could see a wet spot the size of a quarter spread near my fly. I was oozing pre-cum.

Rick squatted. He put his tongue up to the spot and licked. He smiled and sniffed the liquid to pick up its scent. He buried his face in my own stomach, and he yanked my t-shirt up my torso to get a better view of my skinny belly. His mouth tickled me, but I fought the urge to laugh, and when I did, my dick stiffened even further.

He laughed too, and he winked at me. His smile spread wide. Hell, it wasn't even a smile. It was a grin.

I saw a couple of cars drive by, their headlights washing over us, but no one had spotted us. Not yet, anyway. I felt alive and raw, and I wanted more.

And then he peeled open my button fly, and he put his perfect lips up to my shaft. He ran his tongue over every surface, and he probed my balls with the warmth of his mouth. His muscled shoulders rolled back like a bird spreading its wings. He had the length of my dick in his mouth, and he worked his lips up and down, fast, then slow, always just right. He had most of its length in his mouth, and I felt electricity surge up my spine. It was the best blowjob of my life. I wondered what he might be like in my bed, with me on top of his muscular body, kissing, sucking, maybe fucking.

It was all too good to be true, but there wasn't much time for that thought. Everything felt good, and I could feel a tingle at the soles of my feet. I was going to cum. The air blew trash down the street, and I felt like that trash. I wanted to be rolled over, tossed, funneled away by this man's perfect mouth on my penis and his large hands pinning me down onto the car.

He grew tense then under his shirt and he broke out in a deeper sweat, his face gleaming, his shirt soaked.

"You've got to let me fuck you," Rick said.

He stood up again, and I looked up at him, trying to memorize every detail of his face. He had a mole on his right cheek. His jaw was hard and square, like a lantern.

"Sounds good," I said, except I wasn't sure at all. And what kind of idiotic response was *sounds good?* I wanted to slap myself across the face.

I really wasn't sure about getting fucked.

I had only tried getting fucked once, and it had been a disaster. But something in me wanted this tonight, especially with him. He unbuttoned his shirt a little more, to cool off, and the hard muscle of his body ripped through. His pecs were chiseled and huge, mounds of gym-earned muscle, smooth. His stomach was flat and hard, and the sheen of sweat on its surface contoured his abs, his perfect abs. Abs that I wanted to sink my face into. Sweat covered his collarbone. I remembered every comic book hero I had worshipped as a kid, every panel showing off these tight muscles, and I knew he would look perfect in a superhero uniform.

But I was too afraid to bring up superheroes again. If I did, I knew Rick would run away. He had told me was into the same kinky fantasy, but I did not believe him. There was only one person in the world that was simply the best at sabotaging my plans, and that person was me.

Rick took half a step back and pulled down his jeans and revealed a trail of hair that led down to the tight waistband of his underwear, a shiny red pair of briefs that looked all too much like a Speedo. So hot, I thought. I loved Speedos, and this guy wore one under his street clothes. It was fucking bold, and so hot.

He pulled down the red spandex and I got a glimpse of his cock. Not all of it. But just enough. It was a hard and long cock, veined like marble. Uncut, with a large head. He pressed his body on top of mine, and I almost slipped off the hood of his car. He ground his hips into mine, and he repeated, "I need to be inside you."

"Out here, in the street?" I said.

"Wherever you want, however you want." He ran his hand over my neck, and as it moved over my face he clamped it over my mouth, as if to shush me, but hard. I wasn't expecting it to happen, but my dick sprang up harder each time he applied more pressure. I waned those big hands on me always, tonight, and maybe forever. He glanced to each side, looking out for passersby who might catch us in the dark. I saw none, but it was hard to get a good view.

We kissed some more.

Then, a shadow crossed his face, and the intensity behind his eyes changed. He pulled his shirt closed. The wind whipped through the trees, getting stronger. A helicopter cut through the clouds in the distance, close to the farmhouses. He glanced at his smartphone.

"Didn't realize how late it is. I can't stay out tonight; I have to catch a flight early tomorrow," he said.

I was angry. Why was he teasing me like this? I wanted to make this moment extend all night, and now, he wasn't going to finish the blowjob, or anything else that came after that. I could see the red briefs disappear as he zipped up his jeans and ran a hand through his hair. My cock was still erect, wanting more of those red briefs and the heavy balls and cock that lay underneath them.

"You have my number," he said. "You don't just have to text me, you can call me. I am in town for business twice a month."

I was a shy person, but shy people get angry, too. I was angry, and I am not sure why, but I had to say something. I couldn't keep quiet.

"This isn't fucking fair," I said. "This was getting so... good."

"That's why I have to run, because it was so good, and I think you have what it takes to... make it good. There is something different about you, and it's hot, and it has... *potential*," he said.

Rick pressed his shoulders into mine, and he kissed me so deeply I ran out of air. I pushed my own body back into his. He was strong, but I had some strength of my own, and I wanted him to know that I meant this kiss, and that my dick, still hard and pressed up against his thigh, was not going to be satisfied until it got what it needed from him.

But I also knew how a night like this one would end`. He was never going to call me back, and it was never going to be more than a quick blowjob and a grope in a side street of Kansas City. He'd go back to Seattle, New York, or whatever city he worked from. He said he worked in the advertising industry. I made sure to remember what his face looked like, so I could tell my friends this story one day. I had this last chance to see his face, since I would never see it again.

He pulled away from me and got into his car, his muscled glutes flexing as he sat down low in the seat. He rolled down his window and smiled as he sped away. I buttoned up my shirt.

When I got home, I showered and brushed my teeth. I got into bed. In the dark, I ground my hips into my bed and bit down onto my pillow, imagining Rick on top of me, both of us suited in tight superhero uniforms, our skin slick with sweat. I remembered his red Speedo under his jeans, and I embellished my fantasy by placing the red suit over his tights, to seal in place his superhero look. His body engulfed me as he bore down on me. In my fantasy, he entered my ass with his uncut dick, and he kissed the back of my neck. As I lay facedown with my hand around my cock, I came right onto my mattress that night.

His name was Rick.

Or so I thought that night. There was so much I still didn't know.

.

CHAPTER 2
ROOM 808

After the night with Rick, I plunged myself deep into my shifts, my monthly reports, and the budget for the following year at the hospital. It was good getting lost inside these details.

Weeks went by, and one day, as I walked to work, I noticed May had already arrived. Summer was around the corner, and the number of accidents and other mishaps that wandered into an emergency room meant that nurses like me stayed pretty busy. In one day, I had dealt with two kitchen knife accidents, one broken femur, a prescription drug overdose, and a pair of smashed hands at one of the meat-packing plants on the outskirts of town. I had filled out reports and inspected charts. I got no lunch break; instead I worked through it all. Today I would work one of the longest shifts I could remember.

Instead of taking the elevator, I walked up the stairs to get a little more exercise. On my way to the fourth floor, I ran into Roger "Kirby" Kilpatrick. He had just been named assistant administrator of the hospital, but behind the scenes, he ran the whole place.

"Roland," Kirby said, nodding toward me as he walked down toward me. "Looking strong there."

Was he talking about me? Strong was not the word that came to mind when I thought about myself. I was a skinny guy taking the stairs. *Nothing to see here,* I thought.

"Thanks," I said. That was the best I could do to shrug off my sense of awkwardness.

"We need to order you new scrubs. These don't fit you anymore," Kirby said. Kirby stopped right in front of me an put his index and middle finger under the collar of the green cotton. He lifted and the fabric rose almost six inches before the sleeves caught on my armpit. It's true, I was swimming inside the scrubs. The trousers hung off my hips, and if it weren't for the drawstring, they would pool at my ankles.

I felt shame rise up to my cheeks as they blushed. Kirby got a peek at my flat chest under the scrubs, and his eyes invaded me more than I cared for. When he let go of my collar, I sighed with relief. My right leg was shaking.

"Funny you should say that," I said. "I haven't lost any weight recently." It was true. I weighed 155 pounds. My weight hadn't changed in about ten years.

Kirby frowned with a distant sort of disapproval.

"Huh, well, that's strange, I could have sworn it was you that went on that vegan diet and lost all that weight. Hmm," Kirby said. "Must have been someone else."

Kirby was a powerful man, but his corruption and his nasty humor were as legendary as his influence in the hospital. All decisions in the place went through him.

I resumed my climb back up the stairs. I was puzzled by the man's observations. Richards was a red-headed doctor in pediatrics. He looked nothing like me, yet Kirby must have thought that it was me. Richards had indeed lost about twenty pounds recently, and now he looked as slim as I did, but—

Let it go, Roland. It's not worth the mental effort. The man insulted you, but you gotta move on.

My inner voice was right. I didn't have time to think about Kirby. I had to get back to work. I reached the landing and pulled open the door when I heard Kirby shout behind me.

"It was Richards! Now I remember," he said. I glanced back at Kirby and his designer pinstriped suit as he tippy-toed up the stairs to meet me at the landing. Perspiration dotted the razor line of his hairline. "You were never fat, of course you weren't. Not sure how I mixed you two up. You're the skinny one: Roland. I just need to think of a good name to associate with your face, and I can keep you two straight... Slim, that's a good nickname for you. Slim. You could use a burger, especially with all this stair-climbing. You've earned it, Slim."

Kirby grinned up at me. He clearly thought he was charming.

"Thanks," I said. But why did I say thanks? For what? For the insult? I hated these exchanges. I always wanted to say something clever and witty, and instead, I ended up with a shrug of my shoulders and a "thanks." I was not going to generate a proper comeback, and besides, there was the work.

I moved on to my patients. I saw seven of them that afternoon, and my mind focused on their needs.

The shift finally ended at around 6 pm, and after almost 12 hours on my feet, I needed to get as far away from work as I could. I was exhausted.

Kansas City summers were a little hotter than I cared for, but I liked to walk back to my apartment sometimes. Walking helped me clear my mind after long shifts. These walks helped me forget the burn victims, the prescription medication false alarms, the shadows of death that crept up on people in the cancer ward, the life-threatening heart attacks that brought men and women to the ER.

I had about an hour before the sun set, and I walked about a mile toward my place, which was just two miles from the Arkum Hospital. My smartphone rang. On the screen, the phone announced the caller.

Rick.

We had met on the dance floor, and he sucked me off in the street afterward. My dick still throbbed with the memories of Rick's hard chest and the trail of fur he had teased me with the night we met. He had been so much larger than me, the owner of a true jock body. Hard muscle and masculinity exploding from his form like a sun radiating energy.

"Good to hear your voice, Roland," he said.

"I wondered when you might call."

"So what happens to the hero?" Rick said. His voice was brassy and deep. A real man's voice.

I walked past a couple of burger joints, and two cars blasted their horns at me. Rick's voice distracted my thoughts, and I walked without paying much attention to where my feet took me.

"What hero?" I said. I was hoping he meant a superhero, but I had to make sure. Even though he asked me about my fetish the night we met, I still felt guarded about bringing up my interest in muscular men in masks, and villains in tights.

"The superhero, the one you told me about," Rick said.

"I never told you about a specific superhero," I said. "I only told you that they kind of... get me off." I had never told anyone about my superhero fantasy, until I met Rick.

"You did tell me. Now be a good boy and *remember*," he said. His voice commanded attention, even over the phone line. He was not asking me gently, he was giving me an order with every word. I wasn't used to hearing orders barked at me. In my job, I was the one who commanded my team, the one who had to use his experience and wisdom to get things done, firmly and fairly. Even difficult patients had to deal with my direct manner.

And yet, Rick was commanding me over the phone.

It was broad daylight, and Rick's orders made my dick stiffen under my jeans.

I walked faster.

Playing Rick's verbal game was an easy way to keep the fantasy (and the memories of his hard body) going. I gathered the best images of the comic books I had read under the covers as a kid, and the most thrilling scenes I had made up on my own. In each one of them I could see the granite chests, the asses hard as steel, the bulges pressing against the tight fabric of the costumes. Rick liked this verbal roleplay, and I figured, it's just a phone call, what do I have to lose?

"I know what happens to the hero," I lied. I was making it all up, improvising to keep him on the line. "He's not a hero yet, but he's on his way. He's just recently discovered he's got superhuman abilities."

Rick paused, and I could hear a hiss on the wireless line that connected us. He must have thought what I just said was utter bullshit. Cheesy as hell. I felt like hanging up before humiliating myself anymore.

Suddenly, I could hear Rick breathing deeply, like a steam engine churning up a mountain.

"Damn, that's hot," he said. "Tell me more. Where are you right now, by the way? Is your dick hard? Mine's so fucking hard."

But I hadn't said anything yet, I thought. How could he be so turned on? Before letting myself believe again that he was yanking my chain, I decided to give him what he wanted. I made up a story that would get him going.

"Well, it turns out this guy is a hero, he's a fucking superhero, but not the way you might think," I said, as I walked past houses and beauty parlors. It was hot as fuck out here. "He's just a normal guy, but you see, he has a secret. He was accosted by a secret military group when he was in the army, and they injected him with a powerful mutagen. It happened so long ago he forgot. But his DNA was changed forever. As a result, the mutagen altered his cock."

I was enjoying this. I had a full erection now, and if I walked fast enough, I needed move past the people on the street without having to draw their attention. My feet danced on the concrete sidewalk. I felt filthy, gross, and like a fucking pervert. I looked over my shoulder to make sure none of the doctors, nurses, or other staff from the hospital might be near me, listening.

I was hard as hell. My brain was on fire.

"And who is this hero?" asked Rick.

I considered the answer. I could have made up a name, or I could have used any of the alter egos from Arbor, Liberty, or Titan comics, the most famous comic book imprints of all time. I could have simply used the identities of any of the heroes I had grown up with and jerked off to since I had hit puberty. Their names were all there in my memory to choose from: The Fighter, The Overfiend, Aracniss, The Pharaoh.

Instead, I said, "The hero is me. The hero is named Roland."

Roland is my real name. I have no idea why I thought this would make a good name for a superhero, but I didn't want to lose the tension that I felt between Rick and me. And besides, it was just a silly story, improvised. He was just a stranger, really, one who I had barely groped outside in an alley, but it also felt good to put my name to the story he was asking me to tell.

"Good," he said. His voice was full of gravel, rough and manly. A tough voice. It was nothing like my own voice, which sounded lighter, more musical. He growled into the phone again. "Roland, I want you to tell me what you see in the street. Use your super vision, and tell me what you see."

Rick's order made me hard as steel under my briefs. I was sweating buckets, and my shirt was soaked. His voice made me follow its every command. I had never been ordered around like this before. My stomach muscles felt tight, and my legs and arms felt tense, like steel wires.

"I see an empty lot, a strip mall, and on the next block, a gas station."

"I want you keep your eyes on that gas station, Roland. You're going to follow every instruction I give you step by step. If you want to get off today, it's important that you follow every command I give you. Understand?"

Yes, I thought. *YES*.

YES.

"Yes," I said.

"Yes what?"

"Yes, boss," I said.

"No, you mean yes, *master.*"

"Yes, master," I said.

When I said master, my dick strained, trying to break free. My balls ached. Sweat dampened the back of my shirt.

Nothing, and I mean nothing like this had ever happened to me before. Not in my wildest dreams. I felt like every driver passing by was looking at me to inspect my derelict nature. I felt like I was breaking a rule, a rule of propriety. I felt filthy.

I could see the gas station up ahead. It was the old kind, with rusty nozzles and grease streaks on its windows. This gas station had never been touched by the big oil companies. It was a shithole. The kind that had scary bathrooms on the side or in the back. The kind where unfortunate people ended dead, beaten, mutilated, sometimes burned. Nothing good ever came from places like this one.

"Does that station have a bathroom?" asked Rick.

"Yes, it does," I said. I could see it closer now. The bathroom door's sign had once read "men," but it had faded away to green smudges, and the white paint was streaked with grime and black grease. I walked toward it.

"I want you to go in the bathroom, but make sure you don't lock the door," Rick said.

The bathroom itself was nothing more than a narrow box with a cracked toilet and a stained sink. The stains on the walls were revolting. I could hear the ringing sounds of the cash register right through them, as well as a customer asking to fill his own tank. If I was too loud in here, they could probably hear me.

"Roland, the hero," Rick said. "You look good, good for a superhero. You are making me so hard. You have special powers, dontcha, Roland?"

I looked at myself in the mirror. What I saw was the same narrow body I had always known. Smooth arms, clean-shaven face, blue eyes, and blond hair. Runner friends envied this body. I didn't run, but I did enjoy swimming. This body was plain as hell. Weak. Reed-like.

"Look at yourself," Rick ordered. "Lift your shirt up, look at your flat stomach. Feel your hard pecs." I did so, and following his orders made me harder. My fingers traced my chest and my abdominals. All of it was flat as stone. My dick ran down the leg of my jeans, and it throbbed so much it was starting to hurt. My balls ached to cum.

How could he know I was so turned on by his orders, by the texture of his voice? I relished every order that he spat at me.

"Take your shirt off, Roland."

I did. The lean body in the mirror stared back at me. Smooth and hairless, too. *Just a twink man, you're nothing but a twink.* A body that made me uncomfortable. I felt too lean, too small, but—

"Your body is perfect. I am going to get that body on its knees, and that perfect body of yours will be mine. I am going to fuck you," Rick said.

I was panting now, dreaming about his hard-muscled body pressed against me, about his mass bearing down on me someday, slamming me up against a wall, with his cock drilling into my hole while I moaned into the wallpaper. He would ride me hard, and I would be his property. He'd pound my hole, and his cock would be veined, thick, and perfect. I imagined that I might be wearing a blue wrestling singlet, with his dick tearing a hole in the ass to fuck me. I took my fantasy a step further. Maybe he could fuck me with him dressed in a full-body spandex uniform, the uniform of a superhero. And me, I would also be covered in lycra, the material stretching over me, covering every inch of my body–

"You dream of that torso in a superhero's uniform, don't you?" Rick said. He was already two moves ahead. His words became denser, more serious. He commanded a response.

"Yes, I do," I said. I felt like he could read my thoughts, like he could feel how hard he was making me, and how much harder I got while thinking about being fucked in gear.

"Now lower your pants and take them off. Then tell me what you see in the mirror."

I took my jeans off and they slid down my legs easily, the belt clanking as it hit the tiles on the floor. In front of the mirror I could see my hairless body, the pale cream of my skin.

I wasn't wearing my normal underwear. Today I wore my special underwear. This was the underwear I wore when I wanted to feel something smooth and tight against my skin all day. Especially on a long work day. These blue spandex shorts trapped my cock in their stretchy fabric.

They were actually long swimming trunks, jammers, as the swimming pros called them. This pair was royal blue, and tight on my skin like a thin membrane. Shiny and metallic at the same time, the waist held in place by a white draw cord. They conformed to every contour of my thighs and my firm ass. My cock threatened to burst through them.

"I know your secret," Rick said. "I know you are not wearing conventional underwear. You're wearing something special, and I know you have been wearing this special garment more often since we met."

He was right. This was my third time wearing these jammers since our meeting. These blue jammers helped me remember that night with Rick when we had met at Fortress.

"I have. I am wearing swim trunks right now," I said. I no longer cared if the gas station attendant on the other side of the wall could hear me. "Spandex like this gets me real hard, sir."

There it was, that word. *Sir.*

"Good. You're going to give me a special show, boy," Rick said. I could hear the roar of semi trucks pulling into the parking lot of the gas station. It was hot in here, and it reeked of piss. "Now make sure you step out of your shoes and socks. I want you only wearing that special swimsuit."

"Yes… sir."

"Now, take a picture of yourself in front of the mirror. Send it to my phone. This will be the picture you will always remember before you transformed, before you became a superhuman. Just you in your jammer trunks, your bare skin ready for me to suck on it. Ready to move to the next level of your evolution."

Rick's words felt a little silly, because I had never spoken my superhero fantasies out loud to anyone, not even to my former boyfriends. But he said them with conviction. He implied I would be transforming in this bathroom, and the thought of it stirred my cock and tensed my stomach muscles. This was like the classic telephone booth, my place to change into a secret identity.

What was happening here? What was I doing?

My fantasies were coming true. No need to stop the fun.

I steadied the phone's viewfinder, making sure that my whole body was visible, and snapped the digital shutter. The tiles chilled the soles of my feet. I looked at the picture I took. My face looked flushed, and the boner in my trunks looked like a lead pipe. It was the image of a college swimmer ready for a meet.

"Now," Rick said, "You're going to open the door, step out into the parking lot, and stroke your dick until you cum. Then you'll step back inside the bathroom and pick the phone back up to tell me you finished."

My heart beat faster.

I wanted to scream *no* into the phone. I could be caught by anyone in the lot at this hour, even if this gas station was not well trafficked. I would be laughed at, maybe even beaten by some homophobic hick. Rick had no idea what a bad idea this could be. He was from LA, and he didn't understand that even in Kansas City, gossip could ruin a person. I wanted to stiffen my voice and say no, I will not do this.

I put my hand on the doorknob, turned it, and walked out into the lot.

The sun was already setting, and orange light filled my eyes and burst into the bathroom. I walked out into the back lot of the station. Though I could hear the trucks roaring on the road, there was no one back here, just me, facing the empty lot and the woods. I could smell tree sap, and the shadows looked thick between the trees. I was so scared.

What was I doing? This was so... dangerous. And stupid.

But I was hard as fuck, and I was even harder every time Rick commanded me over the phone. All seven inches of my dick were hard as a steel rod, and my balls, round and lightly covered in hair, were filled with cum, hanging heavy. This kind of hard-on reminded me of the ones I used to have when I was 14, jerking off to comic books in the bathroom. Those were hard-ons that almost hurt.

I wanted more of Rick's voice. In fact, I craved that voice again close to my ear. His voice was a drug. I wanted to know what else he could ask of me. But first, I had to follow his orders, and I was ready, because my cock was waiting to cum.

I took two steps onto the dirty asphalt and caught a snatch of rap music in the air. There I was, a registered nurse, in nothing but a pair of spandex jammers, with a long boner., sweating into the evening, and arching my back as I jerked off. I felt danger, but I also felt a deep satisfaction. I put my hand down my waistband and grabbed the shaft, and I stroked. I could feel my mushroom head rub up against the lycra. My back arched a bit as I pumped harder and with more intensity.

I wanted to cum quick, but now, as I stood out here with the sun striking my chest, I felt extremely... deviant as I stroked my cock for any stranger to see as they walked around at this gas station.

A strobe-light memory burst in my mind. I remembered Rick's thick and muscular pecs, the bulge in his pants on the night we met. I remembered his cleft chin and his green eyes. I could see images of fucking, and for a moment, he was fucking me, but then I was fucking him. It was all bursting with colors, some of them blue like my swimsuit, and my lungs tightened as I drew air. My abs stiffened. I could imagine Rick's soft lips on mine and his stubble get so close, so close.

I came, and the white liquid from my balls shot into my swimsuit, staining it quickly, spreading wide. The orgasm shot through me like a bolt of lightning. I bathed that blue Lycra in milk in that shitty parking lot. The bursts of color splashed in the back of my head as I shut my eyes and my body orgasmed.

I looked around. I took a couple of steps back, closer to the threshold of the bathroom door.

There, down the far end of the lot, a car. Someone had just parked, and they were exiting the car from the driver's side. A man, from what I could tell. He was wearing sunglasses. Dark jeans and a short-sleeved shirt. He turned my way, with no purpose in particular. I do not know if he was specifically observing, me, but it sure felt like he was. I was certainly visible to him. My cock grew hard again, thinking about this stranger seeing me in my secret gear, stained with semen, in the doorway. But I felt embarrassed, too.

The stranger put his hand on his crotch to let me know he was cruising me, to let me know he had seen me. I felt shame and embarrassment, but my dick was still hard. I yanked up my spandex shorts and retreated into the bathroom. I shut the door. Inside, I was encased by the stench of the old piss and bleach, and desperate sweat. I took a further step back into the stained room and shut the door. I locked it.

The phone lay on the lip of the sink. I knew Rick would be there on the other end.

"I am done, sir." The words felt so good coming out of my mouth. I was panting, and my heart pounded, rattling my chest.

"Good," he said. "Now, send me one more picture before you put your clothes back on. I want to see those cum stains and the look of humility on your face as you follow my orders." He hung up.

I did as he asked. I knew I shouldn't send naked pictures of myself via cell phone, but I did so anyway. I cleaned up some of the cum off my shorts, but they were completely stained. I cleaned up some of the cum using some paper towels, zipped up my jeans.

When I hit send, I felt good. My scalp tingled.

When I walked back out onto the lot, a strong breeze hit me, and I could see night had begun to fall. The guy who had seen me come out was gone, and so was his car. I could see a wet spot form on the zipper of my jeans and decided to get home fast, before someone saw me. My heart was racing fast, and my mouth tasted of metal.

By the time I reached my apartment building, I was sweaty again, and my jeans were showing more stains. I crossed a few people on the street, but they didn't pay much attention to me, and I doubted they saw the blooming wetness on the crotch of my jeans.

I was about to put my key into the lock to my apartment when my cell phone rang. It was coming from Rick's number.

"We're not done, yet, boy," he said.

"Like hell we are," I said. "I have to sleep so I can work tomorrow," I said. Though I had gotten aroused by the gas station incident, I felt tired, hot under the collar. The game was over.

The heat was pressing down on my temples. I needed some down time.

"Oh, no, don't even bother putting the key in the lock," Rick said. "I'm in town, for business."

"That whole time you had me jerk off at the gas station, you were here?" I said. My heart was beating fast again. I was outraged, and scared again.

"That was just a test. Now we're ready to really play. Meet me at my hotel tonight at nine. Room 808. Door will be open. Bring your spandex gear. I'll have some surprises for you."

"Fuck!" I screamed, and I slammed my hands on my kitchen counter. I had to work, I was exhausted, and I just wanted to sleep. After the longest shift of my life, he thought I was just going to jump through whatever hoop he set up for me?

He hung up.

◆

An hour later, I parked my car about a block away from the hotel. The building towered above me in the night, its diamond lights flooding the sidewalk. I wasn't intimidated by luxury hotels, but tonight I felt out of place. My face was grimy, and my neck was caked with sweat. I still wore the spandex shorts that got me so turned on under my trousers. They remained stained, though they had dried, and I could feel the sticky crust rub up against my cock and balls. I didn't like wearing such soiled clothes, but something inside me told me I had no choice. Something told me that Rick wanted it this way.

Indeed, there was no real choice. I hadn't seen Rick in person since we hooked up weeks before, and now that he had made me strip to my shorts and jack off in public earlier today, I knew he had raised the stakes. I tried to ignore the curious glances of the lobby attendant and the concierge. I am sure I made a decent impression with my clean-cut, lacrosse-player looks, but I felt filthier than I ever had in my life. She glared at me, but I held my head up high and walked on.

I rode the elevator up to the eighth floor. I found room 808 at the end of the hall.

It was now or never.

You can turn right around, go home, shower, keep yourself out of trouble.

It was true.

What if he's a serial killer or a con artist? Better to turn around, and fast.

I put my hand up to the door and knocked. Room 808.

Too late.

"Hello?" I asked, and I could only hear the hum of the air conditioner. I crossed the suite, in which one room led into another. I passed the living room, and then a study. I walked past the bedroom. At the far end of the bedroom, I saw the bathroom. I wandered in and found it empty, except for a black wrestling singlet on the counter next to the sink. Goddamn, singlets got me hard. Their tight polyester or nylon pressed against the bulges of hot wrestler jocks. How I wished I owned one. I ran my fingers over the smooth spandex, and I wondered if Rick had worn it.

Had Rick left this for me? I considered trying it on, but no, there was no note from him. Nothing. I wandered back to the suite. There was another room with a living room set and a flat-screen television that stretched across the wall like a black flag.

There was no sign of Rick. Maybe he had stepped out into the hall to get ice. Maybe he was on the phone in the lobby. Maybe he had forgotten I was coming? Impossible.

I was getting hard thinking about Rick and his dark good looks, his full lips, from a country far away from this one. His meaty arms and his tight, muscular, flat belly. I felt intoxicated by this adventure. I had just stripped in a gas station earlier today, and here I was now, in this man's hotel room.

Should I wait for him on the bed? Maybe I should sit on one of the chairs. I rubbed my hands up and down the leather armrests, but soon I became restless. I couldn't actually just sit and wait.

I walked back into the bedroom, pushing the double doors open behind me. There, on the bed, was a man's dress shirt. It must have been Rick's. He was here. I smiled, glad to know I'd be close to him—

And that's when two arms grabbed me from behind. They pressed down on my flesh, and there was a deep pressure on my arms, my chest. The two arms were vices. A hand, heavy as a bag of cement, clamped down over my mouth and my jaw. I felt air rush into my nostrils as my breathing sped up.

Hot breath washed over the nape of my neck, and the attacker twisted one of my arms behind me. Pain burst through my back muscles and my neck. I tried shifting my weight onto the balls of my feet to get a bit of leverage to escape, but my feet were clumsy. The soles of my sneakers slid on the carpet.

My attacker changed his grip and put me in a headlock. One arm choked me at the neck, the other bore down on the top of my head partially blocking my vision. I let out a moan, which went nowhere except into the crook of the man's forearm and bicep. I could feel his solid muscles pressing behind me, and what might be a weapon, like the tip of a handgun, pressed against my lower back. That tip dug hard into my skin. It could have been a gun, could have been a cock.

"Shut the fuck up, and you won't get hurt, boy," the man said, and he

22

dimmed the lights around me. My belly fluttered. Where was Rick? Had he been robbed by this attacker? I struggled against the hold, but it was too tight.

I looked down, and I saw the attacker's forearm wrapped around my neck. It was like a boa constrictor, squeezing harder with each second. I got hard. My chest filled with fear and my heart raced, but something about the headlock aroused me. "Where's Rick?" I managed to scream through the hand gag.

"Shut up, bitch," the man said, and a rag slid over my mouth and nose. I could smell a scent like rubbing alcohol, but also like mint and lemon peels. My eyes opened wide, and the hotel suite began to look like a prison. The curtains were drawn shut. If I died in this room, no one would know until it was too late.

I kicked as hard as I could, hoping to nail a foot in his balls and escape, to just get a single break for the door. Instead, the man tightened his grip. I screamed harder into the rag. I was hard as fuck but scared for my life, too. I could feel my cock and balls slide around the tight spandex shorts, the same ones that Rick had forced me to stain with my own cum. I wasn't strong enough to fight back.

The chemical on the cloth only blurred my vision, but I remained conscious. I tried to swat at the air with my hands, hoping to free myself by shifting my weight under the chokehold. He pulled me closer to the nightstand, and the lights around me streaked as the chemical went deeper into my bloodstream.

He picked up an object from the nightstand, but it was impossible to make out what it was. It lay in his hand like an instrument, and he brought it closer to my face. The hand and the dark object trailed the air. He put it within inches of my face, and I could finally make out its shape and color. It was a thick syringe filled with an amber liquid, and his index and middle finger were hooked through the steel plunger.

I kicked out harder, but my legs crumpled under me. My dick remained hard under my trunks, but a cold chill ran up my back. Dizziness enveloped my head, and I tried screaming out. The chemical kept me from opening my mouth. The syringe went out of view, and a second later, I felt a prick on the side of my neck. Then a burning sensation spread through from the point of insertion. Whatever was in the amber liquid went into the rivers of blood inside me, and the man's muscular arm tightened around me again, propping me up as I collapsed, but also trapping me tighter.

The smell of tree sap and lemon rind plunged me into a soft place. My eyes grew cloudy, and I felt my chest and legs loosen as I gave into a deep sleep.

CHAPTER 3
A MASTER'S TRUE NAME

I woke up face down on the hotel room bed, with my arms and legs trussed up behind me with a length of material that was taut and strong. I tried slipping my wrists from the bindings, but I could feel it pulling on the faint hairs on the back of my hand. Perhaps it was duct tape.

I had no idea how long I had been unconscious. I was awake, but the hotel room quivered with ripples, still. My head felt swollen, and moving my neck gave me a slight ache.

I remembered the last moments when someone had forced a rag over my mouth. A vague image of a gold-filled syringe drifted in my memory, but then it faded away. It had happened quickly. I had been no match for my attacker, who grabbed me and put me down in a matter of a couple of minutes.

I saw a white bedspread beneath me, and I searched the nightstand for any sign of my cell phone. Nothing. The air conditioning whirred, filling the room with white noise.

I glanced down at my shoulders and saw that I was still wearing my t-shirt. I shifted my hips side to side, to see if I might have been stripped. I could feel my jeans were also still on. Good.

I caught a glimpse of the hotel bathroom off to the right, and though its door was closed, I heard sound coming through it, faint but clear. I don't know how I knew this, but I could also sense the presence of a person behind the white door.

I hoped it was Rick. My dick pressed down on the mattress. I should not be aroused under this kind of danger, but there it was, stiff as a rod. Could Rick have been the person who orchestrated this? Or had I truly been kidnapped?

"Okay, I'm onto your game," I said, taking my chances. "Let me out, okay?" I tried escaping from my bonds, but I wasn't strong enough to rip the duct tape.

I had never been strong, and not physically adept at much. I had been good at getting good grades in school, and good at helping people. That was part of my job, after all. But there were limits to being head nurse at a hospital. I worked long hours, and though my metabolism kept me slim, I lacked physical strength. I swam in my free time, and I had my wits. But I wasn't strong enough to escape the bondage I was in right now. I just hoped my instincts and maybe a bit of that wit could save me this time.

"You will be set free soon, but first, we are going to initiate you, Roland," a voice said from behind the door. "Tonight you will learn what it's like to serve a master."

I considered rolling off the bed onto the floor to try to escape toward the door, but my hog-tie was too good. I might even break my neck falling off the bed if I did so. I was really in a lot of trouble, and the cramps I felt in my shoulders made my fear grow. I was vulnerable. The person behind the door could not just rob me but rape me, hurt me; he could possibly kill me. I felt panic in my gut, and I moaned.

But you're in a hotel room. You can scream. You still have time. Use those lungs, fucker. Escape that way.

I took a lungful of air and let out a bellow as strong as I could muster. I had never been able to figure out how to scream, how to project my voice like a man. I shouted as loud as I could. "Someone! Help me! Get me out of here! Call the police!"

My throat burned and I could taste the chemical that had been used to knock me out. I screamed until my voice tore.

The bathroom door flew open, banging against the wall, and the figure that emerged filled the frame like a shadow, lit from behind by the lights in the ceiling. I could make out the hard shapes of the deltoids in his shoulders, the thick yoke of muscle in the trapezoids, and a tapering shape of a weightlifter, but one that was agile like an animal of prey. The legs were smooth and every muscle incredibly defined.

The figure sprang like a lion. His body was covered in the black spandex singlet I had spotted in the bathroom before. The crotch of the singlet bulged with a dangerously large cock and balls. The man leaped toward my spot on the bed, and my heart shrunk with fear when I saw he had no face.

He has no face. He has no fucking face.

My stomach tightened into a knot. He was going to kill me, and I would never make it out alive from this hotel room.

The man's face was covered in a slick black material. I could only see the shape of his strong cranium, the ridge of his forehead. But the rest was blackness. No mouth, no eyes. He was shouting back at me, even as I screamed. The shout was wordless; it was simply the roar of a beast.

The man lunged. His arms gleamed with sweat, and the grunts he made beneath the mask were full of hate, full of hardness. I was still screaming as he lunged.

It only took him two or three strides to run from the bathroom and leap onto the bed. He landed on top of the mattress and his chest and arms fell on top of me, hard, plunging me into the bed. I screamed, and I saw his face come close to mine, its surface tightly bound in the black material, his heaving chest sweating through the slick fabric. I tried wrestling myself away, but I was tied up and in no position to fight. He took both hands and pressed my face into a pillow. He then pulled me away so I could breathe, and he clamped down his large hand over my mouth.

"Quiet, slave. Don't want to let the neighbors know there's elves between the walls, do you?" he said.

He slapped my face and it stung like fire. The black mask floated in front of my eyes.

My back muscles tightened, and I felt chills run down my back in fear. He turned me slightly sideways so I could face him, and I got a better look at that wrestler's physique and the strong neck crowned by the black mask.

"You shout one more time, and you're walking out of here black and blue, dick smashed and balls punched. Keep it up and you won't make it out of the room at all."

The stranger's voice dominated with every word. Though I wasn't sure why, I liked hearing him take control. I felt my life was on the line, and yet my shaft was hard, my balls tight with sexual anticipation. His weight bearing down on me showed his control over me. I had never been this vulnerable under the weight of a man's body.

He had me pinned under his meaty biceps. I could smell his sweat. A man's smell.

"You'll know when your master is near you, even when you can't see him, you understand?" the mask said.

"I don't know what that means. Explain yourself. Who the hell are you?" I said. I didn't want to die without some answers.

The face leaned in close and kissed me. There was not much to kiss, except the mask, but I had no choice. I was kissing back through a membrane of fabric, but it felt like no fabric I had ever touched. I was reminded of spandex, rubber, and in a strange way, glass. It was slick and reflective, like onyx, but up close and on my lips, it was soft, too. I had never kissed someone hooded like this, but I hardened under my shorts, and I moaned with pleasure for a moment.

I know who it is. It can only be him.

"Rick," I said. "It's you, Rick."

He pulled away from me for a moment. He cocked his head. He was a predator evaluating his prey.

"Do you know how to serve a master?" the mask said. "I will show you the way. But first, our protocol. When I address you, you will say 'yes' or 'no, master.' Understood?"

"Yes, master," I said, not understanding how the words came so easily from my lips. I could feel my dick press against the crotch of my jeans and rub close to his thigh. "Yes, master," I repeated.

"Before you know my words, you will know my voice."

"Yes, master," I said. I tried to get a glimpse of the eyes under the mask, but the black surface told me nothing. I could see myself vaguely reflected in its glossy surface. He adjusted my shoulders to prevent me from pinching a nerve, and he straddled for a moment, towering above me. The white ceiling made him seem gigantic, and his mask was like an eclipse, black against a field of white. His pecs dripped sweat onto his singlet.

The masked man groped his hard-on through the tight singlet, and I could see his muscle flex as he did so. His boner shot straight to the left, and he massaged it with the palm of his hand. I couldn't hear his breathing through his mask, but I could see his chest heave up and down. He grabbed his cock with his left hand, and with his right, he grabbed a patch of the singlet and curled his arm. The material stretched, elongating like taffy. It began to rip, and his muscles grew harder. He ripped the crotch away, and his cock sprang free. It was a monster cock, ten inches long, uncut, just like I remembered.

It has to be him.

"Suck my cock, slave," the man commanded. His hand let go, and my mouth was free. But I knew that if I screamed, he'd gag me again. His cock floated before my face, and I could see the balls anchoring his shaft. I wanted that shaft.

I put my lips on it, and I began to suck. My arms were cramping under the tape, but I didn't care. It felt good to take that cock in my mouth, and it tasted clean, masculine, like minerals. With my face close to his body, I could see the tense abs shift underneath the shiny spandex of his singlet. I could feel his thighs rub up against me, and I my cock ached. I took the length of it as best I could, and I slurped back my own spit as I took him in. His cock was thick and veined, and my tongue worked its way under the head, making him moan with pleasure, and making my own body crave his touch. It was a touch I couldn't get while I was hog-tied. Trussed up like this, I was nothing but a machine made to serve him, to pleasure him. I could feel the masked man tense up, and his shoulders flexed. I could tell he was close to coming.

And then he pulled his dick out of my mouth.

He ran his fingers over my wet mouth and slid his thumb over my cheek, tracing it with my spit and his pre-cum. "Good boy," he said. He slapped me again, this time a little gentler.

He stepped off the bed and stretched his arms. His body was fucking perfect, and the thought of what it might do to me sent fear down my chest. His cock stood erect in the hole he made in his singlet. He grabbed the edges of the hole with both hands, and with one single move, he ripped off the spandex, stripping himself naked. His bronzed body gleamed, just like his black mask did.

He stood before me in silence, and he grabbed a condom from the nightstand. The condom was black, like his liquid mask, and he rolled it on. He leaned over, and I expected to be spanked, or slapped. But instead, I felt the bonds around my ankles loosen. My feet were free. I wriggled my toes to get the cramps to vanish. He pinned my feet with his hands for a second.

"Try kicking out and you're dead," he said. My arms were still taped behind my back, and I was face down on the bed. Vulnerable.

I heard shuffling behind me, and then he slid a wet substance onto my ass, going deep with his finger.

It's lube. Oh jesus, this can't be true. He's going to—

The mask's muscled body landed on top of me, knocking the wind out of me. I felt like a pinned wrestler. His body was warm to the touch, and I wanted to be naked now, so I could feel his skin on mine. I felt awful for being turned on by this attack, but my genitals were on fire with excitement.

"I'm gonna cut your clothes off. Sit still and we won't break skin," he warned.

He pulled a pair of black scissors from the nightstand. In a series of minutes, the masked man had cut my shirt, jeans, and belt right off me. I was in nothing but my blue jammers, face down. My ass exposed and up in the air.

"Remember this moment. Remember I am the master," he said.

I felt his rock-hard hands yank down my shorts over the mounds of my ass cheeks, and down to my knees. And then he plunged his dick into me.

He went in with force and some speed, and at first I thought it was going to tear me apart, but there was a touch of gentleness, too. I felt that warm shaft sliding into me, and my nerves awakened with pleasure. Inch by inch, his shaft went in deeper. I bit down on the comforter as my ass went up and down with pleasure to meet his thrusts. He fucked me long and hard, and now that I was stripped down, I could feel his muscled pecs and flat belly iron me down into the bed while he pounded me.

He thrust his hips in a rhythm, and with each pounding, my insides came alive with pleasure. It was a good cock. I felt myself slipping into deep relaxation, despite being bound like an animal. I wanted to cum soon, and I felt like I could lie under him forever.

And then, he stopped fucking me. He pulled out, and I let out a groan of pleasure as I felt his whole length emerge from me.

"You've had enough, boy. This is just the beginning," he said. He came around to the side of the bed, where I could see his mask up close. His neck was incredibly strong, as if cut from marble. I could smell his sweat, and there, like a shadow, his large cock, dangling, wrapped in its black condom. He kissed me again, and I kissed the mask back, wanting more.

He pulled away and dimmed the light to the lowest setting. Then, sitting there by me, he peeled the mask off.

It was Rick. Same cleft chin, same wavy hair. Handsome.

He peeled off the condom and stuffed his dick back in my mouth again, and I worked my lips up and down for a few more minutes of bliss. He pulled out again.

"We'll continue this soon," he said, and he kissed me softly and with tenderness, on my lips. He rubbed my shoulders and my ankles where the tape had cut into my skin. "I'll take good care of you, superhero."

I remembered how he had pulled on me the night we met at the nightclub. I had shared my fetish for superheroes, and he had left me wanting more. My naked body was now under his control, and his muscles, his black singlet, and his black mask brought back the memories of superheroes and their archvillains. But I had been too scared, and frankly, so turned on from being tied and fucked, that I had forgotten Rick's promise to fulfill my fantasies. And now he had.

He got dressed and stood there in the soft light, towering over me.

"I'm going out for a drink, and when I come back, you'll be gone. You'll find a pair of jeans and a shirt for you in the bathroom. You can shower and clean up, too. And when I come back here in two hours, you'll be in your car, headed back home. You will follow every order, slave."

I wanted to say *thank you, Rick*, but I knew I shouldn't. "Yes, master," I said. The words felt right.

He turned his face to me. The roman nose and that hard chin glistened with sweat. His eyes peered deep into me.

"My real name is Nathan," He said. "You've earned that bit of information today, for following orders."

He undid the tape from behind my back, and he walked toward the door of the suite. He walked out.

I lay there, with my hands crossed behind my back, for a few more moments, my eyes adjusting to the dim light. I was free.

Or was I?

CHAPTER 4
THE GAY BONDAGE MANUAL

In the weeks that followed the night I was captured and fucked in that hotel room, I spent as much time as I could trying to understand what had happened to me.

I had made some of the most dangerous choices a person could make. Stupid fucking choices. I didn't even have the excuse of being young. I was 28 years old, after all. I should know better. And yet, I was still here, safe and sound in Kansas City. But how had I gotten here? I had met Rick weeks ago, and he had blown me outside a club. And somehow, over a couple of phone calls, he persuaded me to expose myself in a filthy gas station bathroom, and to meet him in his hotel room, where he had chloroformed me, tied me up, and fucked me while my hands were taped behind my back. Normal people didn't do this, and intelligent people didn't let this happen to them. But I had.

And yet, it had been the most exciting thing I had ever done. The days after the kidnapping, I had gone back to work at the hospital to do my work, but nothing felt the same anymore. I felt changed.

While I worked my rounds at the hospital, I was able to focus my attention to my work. Each patient record I examined, each vein I tapped for IV drips, each medication dispenser I prepared kept my thoughts from falling into the thoughts about Nathan. While I worked, my mind was safe. But when I wasn't working, I returned to Nathan and the things we had done together.

Before I went to work in the morning, in the shower, I slipped on my spandex trunks and relived the experience, remembering the soft bed beneath me while the attacker fell on top of me, drilling my hole. Nathan had been so good at giving me orders, and I had followed. I would masturbate under the shower head slowly, with my eyes closed. I would work up my cock, until I would see rose-colored spots bloom in my vision, cumming into my own hand when the images of my capture replayed themselves. He had clamped his hands over my mouth while pinning me, and I could still feel his smooth skin on mine, his whispers spilling down my neck.

At night, I would look at pornography of gagged guys and relive the night in the hotel room from new angles. I would cum all over my stomach and lick the cum off my hand, as if swallowing my semen might keep the memories of the masked man, of Nathan in his black mask, deeper inside me.

I craved Nathan's hard body, his muscles, the cleft chin. I craved his cruelty, even if I wasn't sure if it was roleplay or real.

In the weeks since, I had grown restless, and my sleep was all fucked up. Some days I slept two hours, and others, I slept for twelve hours, in a deep sleep. I only had my work at the hospital to keep me stable and balanced. There was always the work, and a head nurse like myself had a lot of responsibility. I needed to feel a sense of structure in order to forget my urge to be owned by the memory of my capture. But when I wasn't working and I wasn't sleeping, whenever I got a ten-minute break from a shift, or during my lunch hour, I was looking for clues about Nathan, whose name wasn't really Rick. At first, these small slips of curiosity were limited to a couple of minutes, but soon, I was spending longer and longer investigating Nathan.

My Google searches didn't turn up much, except that his last name was Paulson. Nathan Paulson. He worked in advertising, as he had said. He hadn't called me again since the last time we met, when he kept me bound in his hotel room.

I needed to know why I had liked being bound and fucked on that bed, with Nathan's muscular body on top of me.

I knew it was wrong to tie up men, wrong to kidnap them. I knew it was wrong to get turned on by it. But if it was so wrong, why was I hard just thinking about it?

I wasn't particularly religious, and I wasn't usually racked by guilt, but this time, I was. My innocent superhero fetish now seemed wrong and foreign. My kink had led me to make terrible choices.

I should have stuck to vanilla sex, I thought. *Would have been safer.*

My circle of friends was made up of people that cared for me. Vanessa, who worked at city hall, had been my friend since I was eleven. Roger had gone to college with me back in California, and he had come back to work in Kansas City, just like I did. He was gay, too, and he was a good friend. Then there were Tran and Vincent, a gay couple who lived in the suburbs and invited me over for dinner on the weekends. All of these friends were people I could count on. But I couldn't tell any of them about what had happened to me.

There was only person I could think of at this moment that could possibly hear my story and not laugh or call the police for me.

Joel ran Our Lady of the Flowers, a gay bookstore. Our Lady was sandwiched in a strip mall between a Vietnamese joint and a dry cleaner. The parking lot reeked of exhaust, and the sidewalk kicked up a cloud of dust whenever a truck rolled by, but Our Lady was a world removed from the grime of the street. Oak bookcases ran in rows like corn in a field, their corners lined up at 90-degree angles to the carpet. Books filled the space from floor to ceiling, but order reigned on each self and in each alphabetical listing.

Two cats lived atop the shelves, inspecting the store with opaque glances. Chuck and Max.

Joel had owned Our Lady for more than 25 years.

"Girl," Joel said, squeezing the air out of my lungs. "You've come to visit your beloved book crew." He planted a kiss of friendship on my lips. I wished so many times that I could be as carefree as Joel, and I tried my best to relax in his presence, but the fact was, he was a man who was so comfortable in his own skin, he made most other men squirm inside theirs.

My friends Vanessa, Roger, Vincent and Tran — none of them knew about my friendship with Joel. I had met Joel years ago, on a Saturday morning. I had come in looking for a Fighter graphic novel, and I had stayed through the early afternoon, talking with Joel about other comics, including The Fighter, my favorite superhero. I had left with my new Fighter book, as well as a copy of *From Hell* that Joel thought I might like.

That day, I learned that Joel had finished graduate school and chosen the life of a bookstore owner instead of the academic track. In this way, he said, he could live closer to the books of writers like Benno von Archimboldi and collector's editions of *The Canterbury Tales*.

I suppose that if Joe might have been younger, and single, and if he were about 30 pounds lighter, he might have been the ideal boyfriend for me. I had always thought this.

He was handsome, that's for sure. Baby blue eyes and brown hair, and a build that was pretty athletic, but I guess he's what they called a bear. He was thick through the torso, and hairy, too. He trimmed his thick beard with surgical precision, and his buzzed hair gave him a very clean look. He reeked of masculinity.

We took a seat on the leather chairs.

"We can't do this without some coffee," Joel said. He dashed to the back of the store to start a fresh pot. While he scooped grounds into the filter, I glanced at the rows of gay and lesbian erotica books on the far wall. Next to my chair, on my right, I ran my fingers over a leather-bound edition of *The Iliad.* On the shelf beneath it, a narrow book devoted to the Greek number phi and the golden ratio called my attention. Some of the designs on its cover reminded me of the shapes I had seen the night I blacked out after my stabbing. Each symbol rested on top of another, forming new geometrical shapes, suggesting movement and energy, like a building made of geometrical shapes. I glanced at the title on the spine: *Fibonacci and the Lost Geometries.* I was reaching out to pull out the book from the shelf when I heard Joel return from the back kitchen. I yanked my hand back.

Joel returned with two steaming mugs.

"I have a story to tell you," I said.

Joel nodded. I told him how I had met Nathan at Fortress, and the oral sex we had shared out in the street. I told him how weeks later Nathan reappeared, how he got me to debase myself, and I explained most of what he did to me in the hotel room. Some of the details, like the liquid black mask and the rough fuck that he gave me, were very hard to explain. I forced myself to go into these details, I was embarrassed, but Joel listened, nodding his head. When I finished my story, he grunted. He cocked his head and put a hand to the back of his neck.

"It's almost closing time," Joel said, adjusting the sleeves on his shirt, "and you're the only other person in here. Why don't you flip the sign over by the window and lock the door behind you? I have something I need to show you."

We walked to the opposite corner of the store, past detective novels, a shelf dedicated to horror novels, and a row of classics of gay and lesbian literature. Finally, at the end of stack of books, we hit a dead end. Back here, two short shelves near the floor labeled "BDSM" forced us to squat to look the spines over.

I crouched. I could see Joel's thick shoulder muscles bunch under his t-shirt, and his linebacker legs, as he sat back on his haunches. For a moment, I considered what it would be like to feel his thick, furry body up close. I had craved sex for so long, I wondered why I had never taken a closer look at my friend before. In all my years, I had always slept with skinny guys like me, happy to enjoy their angular bodies. But I couldn't possibly be serious, could I? He was virtually married to his boyfriend Adrian. My appetite was whetted, and the thought of a bear's thick shoulders and arms—

Joel snapped me out of my fantasy.

"I can recommend a lot of books from this shelf," he said. "There's plenty of guides to help you get all the kinky sex you want without ending up in jail or mutilated and stuffed in a trash can. What you did with this guy, it could have gone bad, and fast."

"I know," I said.

"But something tells me it probably got you off really good," Joel said while inspecting the books. "I can spot a good perv when I see one.

Welcome to the club, girl; you made it. So, you can look at this shelf on your own, but here, this is the book I'm picking out for you." He pulled out a paperback, time worn and faded. Symbols floated suspended against the black background of its cover.

The Golden Man: A Gay Bondage Manual, it read. The cover did not list the author's name. I turned the book over and found it on the spine. Salvatore Argento.

"This is more of a BDSM 303 kind of book," Joel said, "but you read a lot, and you work in the medical profession. I think you can handle it."

I took the book from him. Inside, the print filled the pages like veins made of ink. A few pages had cryptic diagrams and more symbols, but the book was otherwise a dense tome, filled with pages of text.

"What kind of book is this?" I said.

"There's strange stories out on the street about that book," Joel said. "It's impossible to find it in print anymore, and Google searches only turn up some occasional references. It's been used as a guide for people who want sex that isn't of your garden variety. If you get into leather, bondage, it shows you how to hold on to your power, and also how to give it away. Some of these basic tenets, like negotiating your limits, need to be addressed first. So back up for one minute and tell me, girl: how is it possible you let some stranger stick a needle in you just like that?"

I shrugged. "It was hot" was all I could muster to say. "It scared the shit out of me at the time, but that's all I can think about now."

"So about that," Joel said. "You gotta do what you gotta do to make sure you stay safe, even when you're getting your brains fucked out of you. The book covers some of that."

Joel followed that last sentence by a long stretch of silence, as if he were thinking very carefully about what he was going to say next. He uncrossed his legs and leaned forward in his leather chair. He was so close I could smell the rich, chocolate scent of coffee on his clothes and on his breath.

"There's also *other* uses for the book," he said.

"Other uses," I said.

"Yes. Some people say that the book is also loaded with puzzles."

"Puzzles?" I said.

"Yeah, metaphysical and philosophical puzzles."

"Like a Buddhist koan," I said.

"Yeah," Joel said. "You could say that. Or maybe it's the kind of stuff you might find in an Umberto Eco novel or in a university class on Lemarchand theory. Puzzles made of interlocking words, or puzzles meant for our eyes to see and our minds to imagine. I myself have never found any, but the previous owner of the book said he found not just a handful of puzzles but literally thousands inside the book. He got spooked when he couldn't stop counting them, so he sold me this copy."

"And you believed him?" I said.

"Funny you should ask. I thought he was acting kind of weird. Like he had actually stumbled upon something in this book, kept that information to himself, and now he wanted as much distance between him and the book as possible."

Joel looked away from me and focused his gaze instead on his two cats, perched above the stacks. Chuck and Max's eyes glinted.

"The book is a good guide for protecting your safety, and the safety of the people you fuck." He said. "That's one of the things the book can do, if you can find what it is you need inside its pages."

"If it's so rare, why do you have a copy of it back here, just like this? Shouldn't it be more... prominent? Why is it relegated to shelf in the back?" I said.

"Honestly, because no one has ever asked for it," he said. "I don't think it's all that rare; it's just out of print. And though it may sound strange, it has been taken down from the shelf, but no one has ever purchased it. So there's that. But if you're going to be doing more cowboys-and-Indians with ropes and gags, and you enjoy a roll of duct tape the way a CEO enjoys a good Cuban, you should read it."

Our Lady had always provided me with a comfortable space to come and buy my favorite books, and I had spent many afternoons in this very chair, browsing, comforted by the clean, dry air and the quiet atmosphere. That serene quiet felt wrong now, and though Joel inspired confidence in me, I felt strange under the watch of his mute cats. Even Joel was making me feel uneasy. The dark spaces between books on the shelves felt dank, musty.

I promised Joel I would read the book.

"You shouldn't be afraid of what you're feeling," Joel said. "The husband and I have been playing kinky for years. But we might never have done so, if it hadn't been for the book.

"I opened the store in 1988, but the man who sold me the book didn't walk in through the doors until 1990," Joel said. "At the time, Adrian was a sweet young thing, and so was I. So, when you look around Kansas City now, be glad there's Latins and blacks, and be even more glad that when you go to a gay bar, Latins and blacks are not that big of a deal. But back then, Adrian still drew many stares, and the fact that he was gay, and living with me didn't help all that much to go under the radar.

"So, I had opened the store just a couple of years before, and this older guy walked in, wanting to sell me *The Golden Man*. I figured it was a remnant from the Timothy Leary era. Maybe by some author who wrote a book and then disappeared back into a hippie commune. But the gentleman insisted it was an obscure book by Salvatore Argento, the New England journalist from the turn of the 20th century. He turns up in some pulp magazines of the time, and collectors who specialize in those weird magazines of the time totally get a hard-on for his name. Anyway, the old man was all too eager to get rid of the book, and I offered him a fair price. I paid him in cash, and he took off on foot. 'What do you do?' I asked. 'I used to be a teacher,' he said. I never saw him again.

"Just a week before, Adrian had begged me to tie him up and fuck him. Now, I don't know what kind of whore you may think I am today, but back then, I was wound up tighter than a cuckoo clock. The idea of tying up my big strapping husband to our bed post seemed wrong. Ever read *Helter Skelter*? I had just read it for the second time, and I refused to even go there with the bondage.

"But the night I acquired *The Golden Man*, I took it home. I started to read. The book surprised me, to be honest. As you'll see, the book goes down a certain path, following an idea, but then it seems to hit a dead end. Then it backtracks, and it takes you in the other direction. You make another few turns, and you find that you're somewhere very, very far from where you started. So far that you start trembling, wishing you knew how to get home. So... that is exactly what happened that night. The book's poetry passages jumped out at me, and in them I found ideas about bondage and domination that I didn't think were possible before. The story of the Eastern Mariner is a prime example. You'll see when you read it; there's a few chapters devoted to it. That story of the Eastern Mariner and the mermen he captured and bound in the Atlantic sparked an idea for me, and I applied this idea to Adrian's request for me to tie him up.

"I knew then that maybe what Adrian was asking of me might be all right, if I considered his request one of power, instead of a plea for pity. Because I'll be honest with you, girl, before I ever trussed up a man spread-eagled on a bed, I found the whole bondage thing silly. Even pitiable. I used to giggle just thinking about it.

"And then there were other corners I turned in the book. The chapters on mathematics and physics freaked me out, and when they didn't, they sort of put me to sleep. But they say that every man finds a unique jewel inside the pages of *The Golden Man*, and my jewel was in the Eastern Mariner story.

"And through and through, the other stories inside the book, including the bizarro shit that the Golden Man does by the end — oh, don't worry, I ain't spoiling this for you. But you'll see — they reminded me of a book I might read some day in the future, like *House of Leaves,* even though that book was more than a decade away from publication. *The Golden Man* inspired me, and it spooked me a little, too. I have never in my life read a book like it. It's stayed inside me all these years.

"It took me four days to read the book from cover to cover. And on the fifth day, I put it back on the back shelf, where you and I found it today. That afternoon, I called up Adrian at work. He sounded busy, but I didn't care. I asked him what he really wanted me to do when we got home that night. I asked him what his limits were, and I made sure that we both had a signal we could both recognize if it got too intense.

"These dirty things, my little Roland, I had never done before. I was a fine young thing then, and I could fill out a jockstrap better than a college quarterback. I put one on, and I waited for Adrian to come home from the firm. He put down his suitcase at the door, and he smiled. He saw my trim body, my tight jock, and I could see he was getting hard under his trousers. When he came up to me to kiss me, I slapped him across the face. *Not this time, boy,* I said. I spat in his face. And I forced him down on his knees.

"I made Adrian worship my feet, licking and sucking every toe clean until he moaned with pleasure. Then, I collared him and led him on all fours to the bedroom. I ordered him to strip, and I inspected that goddamn perfect black skin of his. Black don't crack, and it's true. He's still flawless today, and he's already in his fifties. The collar was perfect for him, and exactly what he wanted. Now I know what you're thinking: A white man collaring his black boyfriend. How fucked-up is that? That's loaded with problems of race, class, and the whole history of oppression.

"Well, you're fucking right. Damn fucking right. But when I saw the collar for what it was, which was a way for Adrian to fulfill his own deep fantasies, I let go. And I really let go. I tied him down onto the bed, his body splayed out like a pinwheel, and I gave him my cock, my ass, my pits, and my toes. He especially liked the toes. Worship while bound is perfectly hot. I cut the rope at his ankles some slack, and I fucked him hard, spitting in his face, and kissing too. I rode that ass as far as my body would let me. I gave Adrian what he asked me for. That was one of our hottest sessions, to this day.

"I left him tied for a few moments while I smoked a cigarette, and I turned away from the bed to look at myself in the mirror. *Not bad, Joel,* I thought. *Not bad.* That was 30 pounds ago, and my mind was screaming *you're a stud.*"

I was half hard listening to Joel's story, but my cock didn't come to full mast. I felt embarrassed in the presence of Joel's candor. People really talked *this* freely? I was even more confused by the fact that I actually respected and liked Joel. Had he always been this filthy, and maybe I had just never noticed?

"But how does this story make the book that special?" I asked. "It just seems to me like you basically gave Adrian what he wanted."

"I knew you were going to say that," Joel said. "That's why I like you, kid. You make an old bitch feel like a clever fox.

"So, by my count, *The Golden Man* contains probably about 100 different stories, but it's possible there's many more. Some of them lie hidden in meaning, so you really have to know how to read between the lines. But one thing is true. The story of the Eastern Mariner, that hot little handful of poems, not only got me hard, it hinted that sometimes we are not prepared to received what we really want, even when our partners give it to us. Now, that sounds all kinds of movie-of-the-week and shit, but no, it's a little more perverse. In my case, I gave Adrian exactly what he wanted, and in doing so, I realized that maybe I wasn't as prepared as I should be.

"I was still smoking that cigarette while Adrian lay tied to the bed when I realized that there was a hole in the wall. And when I say a hole, I don't mean a little hole where ants can crawl through. No, up in the molding, I spotted a hole the size of a baseball. How I had never noticed before is beyond me, but well, there you have it. And you know me. A hole in the wall can only mean one thing. Mice. Or rats. The longer I looked at the hole, the darker it felt, and the darker it got. Its blackness seemed to seep out through the plaster. Something had made that hole. Something big.

"And so I simply started freaking out. Adrian, I said, have you seen the size of this thing? We have to get someone out to look at this tomorrow first thing in the morning. There's no way I want to sleep in a room with an infestation like this. I'll check the yellow pages, but there is no way in hell we can sleep with a hole like this, where any old creature can just crawl up and—

"I had been talking so long, gesticulating with my Marley Light, that I never noticed that Adrian had wriggled out of the rope, stood up, and crept up behind me. He tapped me on the ass to startle me, and since I was so bent on thinking about mice, I felt a tingle in my ass and jumped. And I screamed. I thought the mouse that had crawled in through that hole was here and now, going up my thigh. And so I screamed again.

"That's when Adrian used his bulk and his height to take me down. We wrestled on the bed, and we tumbled with me on the floor, but by the time he was done with me, he had me collared, and he dragged me by the hair out into the dining room. He tied my hands together and looped the rope over a chair at the far end, while my ass went up in the air for him to enjoy. He took that curved dick of his, and while I still had my jock on, he went in deep, making my eyes water and my cock harden with lust. Our windows were partially drawn, and I could see our neighbors pulling up in their station wagon across the street while my boyfriend tore up my hole so good.

"Now, you have to remember, this was out of the norm for us. This was the first time Adrian had fucked me like this, and he woke something up inside of me. Something deep. As he fucked me, riding me like a pony, I began to scream out things I had never let myself say before. *Stick me with that powerful dick. Come on, feed me your big black dick. Come on daddy, fuck this white-boy pussy, it's all yours. Give me your big black cock. Treat me like your little white slave, like a piece-of-shit cracker. Fuck me hard, you black god, and feed me your black power."*

Joel leaned back in his chair and giggled. He snorted a bit, and he smiled at me.

I didn't know what to say.

"You have to remember, in those days I was a prissy grad student, even though I had just opened my store. And I felt guilty about the words I said to Adrian in the heat of our lovemaking, and I felt wrong. I felt like the biggest piece of shit on the earth. So much talk about black and white, and holy shit, where could I find a therapist who could help me deal?

"And then I remembered to just let it go. Kind of like the book suggested. After all, I had done this consensually with Adrian, and we talked about our limits. We had both agreed on what this depravity was going to be. And afterward, when he removed the collar from my neck, he kissed me hard and long, for about five minutes. 'Thank you for giving me the night of my life,' he said. Later we talked about the race issues, but that's another story for another day. The point is, though, we had a lot of fun. And even though there were surprises, I suppose we were pretty safe.

"So... that brings me to my point. I want you to promise me you're either going to figure out what you want out of your little trysts with this guy from LA, or that you'll just go find some other guy who can tie you up safely without injecting you in the neck and raping you."

"I promise," I said, but my words were flimsy. I knew, and Joel knew it. But I had to say it anyway. I wanted to give my friend a great explanation about why I let myself get carried away by Nathan's reckless ways, but to be honest, I didn't even know how to begin. I began to feel uncomfortable here.

"I gotta get going," I said. Joel's face looked disappointed in me, and I knew that if I stayed any longer, he would call me out on my bullshit.

We walked back to the front of the store. Darkness had fallen over the parking lot, and the glow of the sodium vapor lamps in the street lit my skin in orange light.

"Nowadays, Adrian likes it when I tie him spread eagled-on the bed and stuff my used jock in his mouth," Joel said. "We don't play as much as I'd like, nor as intensely as we used to, but it's not a big deal, really. A hubby does many more things than just stand in as bondage bottom."

That last tidbit of Joel's private life made my head spin with ideas, and this time, I was definitely turned on by his lack of inhibitions.

"How much do I owe you for the book?" I said.

"I told you, it's yours to keep. Don't worry about it."

"I really am thankful to you for thinking of me. I mean it."

"Are you going to let this guy fuck you again,?" Joel said.

I said I wasn't sure. This time I was telling the truth. I may not be ready to be penetrated by Nathan, but I did want to be near his presence again. I wanted to feel his rough hands, and the sting of his spankings.

"Liar," he said. "You're counting the minutes until he trusses you up like a little pig." He laughed again, and he hugged me.

All this conversation hardened my dick, and I shifted my weight onto my other foot to hide my erection from Joel. The man was in his fifties, but his thick body exuded health and vitality. He looked really good. Bears were not my thing, but the thought of him and his boyfriend, one restraining the other, stuffing a bandana in his mouth, and worshiping Joel's nipples, got me hard.

I kissed his bearded lips. I enjoyed the moment that my hand lay on his muscled shoulder. Then I walked out of Our Lady. I waved as I backed out my car and pulled out of the strip mall. Though Joel was smiling, he looked really worried for me.

◆

That night, I began reading the book. I flipped open its pages while I reclined on a chair in my living room, and five hours later, I found myself curled up in bed with the paperback propped up on my chest.

The Golden Man: A Gay Bondage Manual told the stories of various men in different time periods, countries, and states of mind. At first glance, the book stacked up stories upon stories, and they didn't seem to connect. But as I fell in deeper in its text, I noticed that many men (and women) in the book held an inner desire to be controlled, to be tied and bound. Naturally, many others wished for the opposite, to keep a submissive under their control, to own them in some way. This book didn't contain instructions on how to tie a single rope knot. Instead, it just spilled stories, like a cup that has been filled beyond the brim. Some stories were ancient, and some nothing more than lines of poetry. Occasionally, the author retold iconic tales of bondage and domination, such as Samson and Delilah, Prometheus bound to a rock. The book promised beauty through bondage. Something about those words seemed right, though I could hardly imagine what they *meant*.

I reached the middle chapters, which to me were stranger than the rest. In these chapters, the author spoke about legends of a man made of perfect proportions of mind and body, a man who channeled the universe through the matter he took up in space and time. This man could harness the end of the world, and in fact, he could even unleash the apocalypse with his power. He was a man that was feared and revered by organized religions, but a man that was so powerful, he was to remain secret, bound up inside secret symbols in medieval manuscripts, in alchemical handbooks, inside the rhymes of the bards.

He was a man that was destined to be buried in the heaps of the legends that men made up about him. He was known in some places as the Golden Man. Each chapter revealed more about the Golden Man's origins, yet it seemed to me that the more I learned, the less I understood. Anxiety swept over me as I moved on to each new chapter. Terrible events were supposed to follow the Golden Man like a shadow. It was his very presence which sometimes unleashed death, destruction, and famine.

As I read each chapter, I found my boner growing taut and long, imagining how Nathan might tie me up, maybe soak a bandana gag in whiskey and stuff it in my mouth, flog my ass until it was raw, clamp my nipples until my eyes rolled into the back of my head. Maybe he'd fuck me hooded, like he had the night he kidnapped me and abused my hole just a few months ago.

I fell asleep with the book on my chest, and the next morning my sheets were sticky with the wet dreams the stories of *The Golden Man* had induced.

CHAPTER 5
THE SWIMMER

I woke up each morning hoping Nathan would call me. Even just a text would do.

But Nathan only contacted me every couple of weeks. During his phone calls, he liked to talk and play with words, using his deep voice to replay our sexual encounters. Doing this turned him on, and I admit it made me hard, too. I often took his calls while I drove alone at night, or sometimes during my walks in the botanical gardens. Nathan replayed the times he had tied me up, flogged me, bound me to chair for hours while pumping my dick with an electric milking machine. Each time I answered his questions, I added "sir" to the end of my sentences.

And one day, finally, Nathan announced he was coming back into Kansas City for business meetings. He would be staying at the same hotel.

"You know what to do, boy," he said. "Be prepared to serve that night. Come in well rested, your skin washed, your ass cleaned."

"Yes sir," I answered.

That night in late August, we played in his hotel playroom. He had finished his corporate meetings for the week, and he lay inside room 808 once again. I tried peering through the peephole of his room, as if I could get a glance of a sleeping lion inside, before I knocked. "Come in," he said.

I stepped into the room, feeling unlike myself. I had noticed new things about my body, and I wasn't sure if Nathan would notice them.

He inspected me again, circling me like I was prey. He removed all my clothing, and he inspected my nude body. He tapped my ass with his hand, and he squeezed I was not allowed to talk during this inspection. He nodded with approval, and he eased me down onto his bed.

While I lay on my back, Nathan tied my balls and cock with a length of rope.

I took a deep breath and broke my silence.

"*Sir, my chest has hair,*" I said. "Have you noticed?"

Nathan's head popped up from the nest of knots at his fingertips.

"This is making me so hard," Nathan said. "Nothing hotter than a man growing, becoming a muscled god, gorging himself with blood. This is some seriously hot roleplay," he said.

It was true. Ever since the night I had been stabbed, and through the weeks where Nathan drew me into his game of master and servant, I had noticed small hairs sprouting on my chest. I attributed the changes to becoming older, and it made me feel good. I wanted to share it with my master.

But have you noticed, Nathan?

I bit my lip, suppressing my anger. He refused to answer my question.

This isn't just superhero roleplay, I thought. *Why can't you see, why can't you listen? People don't just sprout chest hair at will.*

Nathan was into roleplay, and so was I. And that roleplay had fueled many nights of phone sex. Those were nights that had swelled and exploded in cum, with stories of my imaginary transformation, but all those conversations had taken place across thousands of miles. Nathan hadn't been there to witness the horrors taking place inside and outside my body.

I was different now. Couldn't he see it was real?

I wanted a certain comfort from Nathan, but I didn't know how to ask for it. Maybe this was the truth finally arriving: we had a long-distance relationship in which he would come to visit me in Kansas City and slam me up against the wall when he walked in the door. He tied me down and punished me, but it was nothing more than fucking. Why would I expect him to care about my changes if we only met in person every couple of months?

Nathan ordered me back to standing. He gave me a jockstrap to wear, and he tied me spread-eagled on the bathroom floor of the suite, twisting my balls and nipples until my cock got rock hard and precum stained the white cotton. I could taste his hardness in the red ball gag he would stuff in my mouth. When he spread my legs apart and pushed his cock into my ass, I felt close to him. I felt safe. It was a relationship I craved and a physicality I couldn't live without. After he came, he flogged my chest and stomach, and I felt the heat of a thousand volcanoes under the skin. He undid the rope that held me down. He folded it with care into three neat loops, never breaking eye contact with me. He tucked the rope under his arm and walked out of the bathroom.

I stood up and jerked myself off, caressing the burning red skin on my stomach. With each stinging touch I felt harder and more aroused. I came into the bathroom sink.

I went into the living room of the suite, and I looked out the windows.

He had stepped out into the courtyard of the hotel and smoked a cigarette, alone, staring up at the sky. A half hour later, he returned to the room with a bottle of wine and tender kiss for my lips, the back of my neck.

I understood that this was just roleplay, and that if I wasn't careful, it could be labeled as abuse. We never did negotiate my limits. Instead, I just took whatever he handed out to me.

But the fact was, Nathan had never said a cross word to me outside of the brutal sessions of bondage and spanking that he put me through. He was a gentleman. But I wanted him closer to me. I considered moving to LA, but why? He wasn't particularly interested in making a life together. He seemed just happy tying me, fucking me, leaving me in a pool of sweat and cum on the floor, then taking off again. Hopping on a flight to beat me into submission was easier than actually having to deal with me everyday.

We drank the bottle of wine, and I reluctantly left the hotel suite when it was over. There would be no lounging in bed, no whispers at dawn.

"I've got my eyes on you, boy," he said. "I'll see you next time."

Days passed. I worked longer shifts. I jerked off while stuffing a pair of underwear in my mouth, trying to relive the gags Nathan put in my mouth to keep me quiet. I came into my mattress, wishing for his weight on top of me.

After our meeting in that hotel room, I didn't hear from Nathan for almost a month.

In that time, nature played a sick joke on me. With each day, more changes burned through my body like a forest fire that can never be put out. Behind each change, there was a push, like a boulder stirring in the wind before it tumbles down a ravine.

An unknown force moved inside my body, like a cancer.

When you reduce cancer to its essentials, it's nothing more than an excessive growth of human cells. You don't need to go to medical school to know this.

Cancer had always been around me. It killed both my parents when I was a teenager, and it left me alone in the world. In nursing school, I studied how the organs of the body are affected by the uncontrolled division of cells. And now, in my daily job, I was closer to cancer than ever. It destroyed the bodies of my patients, and in many ways, it destroyed their minds.

The first signs of cancer can sometimes be discharges in bodily fluids, painful tender spots in tissues. Sometimes cancer can be detected in the human form when an organ or limb changes its shape and size in a very short amount of time.

In the past few weeks, the tissues of my body had transitioned from one state to another. There were changes happening internally, but I was too afraid to investigate those with my doctor. The outer changes were easier to spot. The outer changes were, in fact, impossible to ignore.

For example, one day I noticed my left hand was larger than the other by almost three inches. A week later, the other hand had also grown. Soon they were identical in shape and size. The same went for my pecs. Small lumps the size of peas dotted the outer edge of these muscles. Some days the lumps felt hard like pebbles, and on other days softer, like a pencil eraser. And then one day, they disappeared, as if washed away by a solvent.

At other times, I felt lumps under the skin of my forearms. Sometimes I thought my legs were deforming. These changes terrified me, but I became very good at ignoring them. Fear kept me static, and weeks went by as my bone, skin, and muscles reassembled themselves against my will.

If you've ever seen a snake molt from its skin, you can understand how I felt. The snake emerges from its skin, shedding it like a transparent shell. It leaves the former self behind, and what emerges is more colorful than before. Bigger, stronger. The newly skinned snake is now ready to hunt.

The thoughts of snakes crept into my days. When they did, it was at the worst times: during department meetings, at the dry cleaner sometimes while I was sitting in the toilet. I tried shoving the images of snakes out of my mind, but I couldn't help but see their coiled bodies and the curves of their fangs.

Nowadays, my body, though connected to my mind, no longer felt my own.

And there were other changes, too.

Some changes, like the timbre of my voice, were subtle. Over the recent weeks, my throat had lowered itself to a baritone. During my shifts at the hospital, some of the nurses and doctors in my team noticed it. "I have a cold that won't leave me," I would say. I fake-coughed for extra effect. At staff meetings I was quieter now, content to doodle in a legal pad so that I wouldn't have to use my strange new vocal register. Better to not draw attention to myself. Because the voice was just one of many changes.

My change in height was the toughest to ignore, and I could not hide it from the people around me. I had topped out at 5'9" back when I was 17 years old, but now, more than a decade later, I had grown a full three inches in the course of five months. *Three inches in five months, dammit.* My jeans rode up my ankles, and my favorite shirts came untucked as my legs and torso grew. I bought new clothes, but the clothes didn't stop my neighbors from staring at me or our development director from stopping me in the hallway to ask if I was using shoe lifts.

My cock changed. I had measured my dick recently, because I was sure the length of my penis was not seven inches anymore. I measured nine inches now. It looked wider too, denser, as if packed with cement. My balls hung heavy in my boxer shorts. I suspected they had grown, too.

I believed in medicine with all my soul, and I probably should have gone to get myself checked out at the very hospital where I worked. Some tests and a biopsy could possibly help what ailed me. Medical exams would help solve this puzzle, and if I had cancer inside me, the data would show that fact.

And yet.

I considered the cancerous changes of my body as I locked up my file cabinet and shut down my computer. I waved goodbye to the team on duty, ready to walk out of Arkum Hospital. I would drive myself home tonight, and the darkness of my apartment would greet me, envelop me.

On my way down the main staircase of the hospital, I ran into Kirby. "Looking good, Roland," he said to me, tipping his head in my direction.

Every time I was in his presence, I felt nervous and awkward. The only word that came out of my mouth was "thanks."

"You been hitting the weights?" Kirby said.

Before I had to stop and make conversation, I tapped my watch and pointed toward the door. *Gotta go.* As I did so, I blushed. As soon as I did this, I regretted it.

My arm.

My goodness, my bicep was so… big, and so… puffy. So muscled. Kirby didn't seem to troubled by it, but I did. Had it grown in size while I was sitting at my cubicle? I tucked my arm down by my side and got the hell out of there. I walked home.

I folded my work scrubs from the hospital and tossed them in a hamper. It was late on a Friday evening, and I had just about an hour before the public pool closed for the evening. I stepped out of my socks and underwear, pausing for a moment before putting on my shorts and t-shirt.

My image stared back at me in front of the full-length mirror in my apartment. I stood taller and hairier. My skin had been so smooth before, but now I had a thick pelt of fur between the hard grooves of my pecs. It had started out blond, like the hair on my head. Today it was dark blond, shades darker than my original golden color.

My ab muscles looked more developed, and my cock, that longer cock, was coming up to standing position even now, erect thanks to its own reflection. I didn't want to get turned on by my own image, but the fact was, this was a body I had craved for years, and now the fantasy was my reality.

My transformation had started five months before, when I had met a stranger named Rick in the middle of the night, while I drank gin and tonics in a place called Fortress. My Fighter t-shirt had kicked off our conversation, and he had told me he got hard thinking about superheroes. Rick had sucked my cock. Weeks later, Rick had revealed his real name, Nathan. He had also shown me how to serve his needs, and how my role as his submissive gave me pleasures I never knew were possible.

This new body turned me on, and it made me feel strong, virile. But I was ashamed to take it outside this apartment. *I am an impostor*, I thought. *I still feel like an impostor.*

I finished my day shift at 6 pm, and I came home and ate a bowl of cold noodles and drank a glass of beer. I felt restless.

I got my face up close to the mirror. Were my eyes changing color, too?

I didn't like the flecks of color that radiated from my pupil. I felt like my own enemy.

I had to get out of the house that night.

I grabbed a pair of black swim trunks from the drawer in my dresser. I had always been turned on by the guys on the swim team, and I loved the way the tight fabric slid over my legs and ass, the way it cupped my dick and balls, showing off the cut head. This pair was shiny black. I considered jerking off before heading out, but I didn't want to miss my swim. I finished up by putting on some shorts and a shirt, and I went out the door.

◆

The water rushed around me, and with each stroke and each breath, I lost myself. I swam 2,000 meters in the pool. Moonlight cut through the large windows on each side and the trees shimmered. I loved September.

Other swimmers' bodies cut ribbons of water in the lanes of the pool, but after a while, I forgot that they were there at all.

I finished my training with a final lap of butterfly stroke, pumping my body in undulating waves, doing my best to let go of all the anxiety I had accumulated over time. Since I started changing, a sprint like that didn't even leave me winded. I felt stronger.

I emerged from the pool and realized I was the last swimmer left in the lanes.

The lifeguard read from her smartphone while sitting in her chair in front of the bleachers. She looked like my former chemistry lab partner in high school. Maybe she was, I don't know. I walked past her in my Speedo, self-conscious about my chest hair, my swollen arms, and all other aspects of my body. Would she recognize me if it was really that freckled girl from my younger days? She stared at me for a moment, glanced at my body, then resumed tapping at the screen of her phone.

The park district building was closing in another 30 minutes or so, but pool hours were over.

I walked into the locker room. I had never seen it completely empty until now. It lay deserted, except for someone at the farthest end, by the showers. My skin broke out in gooseflesh as the cool air from the ventilation system touched my skin. I caught a side glimpse of myself in the mirror, my Speedo tight around my hips and ass, outlining my bulge. I got half hard feeling the silky fabric on my cock. The swimsuit reminded me of my favorite superheroes from the comics. They always wore trunks like these outside their tights.

I walked toward my locker, which was at the far end of the narrow room. My nostrils took in chlorine and sweat.

There, next to my locker, was the only other swimmer in the pool that night. He was about 25 years old, I guessed. He had a strong build, the kind men achieve when they flip houses on the weekend, installing drywall and sawing two-by-fours. His skin was a light creamy brown, punctuated by a handful of moles on his shoulders. Narrow hips and wide shoulders. His proportions equaled to that of the classic swimmer's build. He didn't wear a Speedo like I did. Instead, he wore baggy shorts. Despite them, I could see he had a nice tight ass beneath. He was busy rummaging through his bag inside the locker, with his back turned to me.

He turned around when he heard me open my locker. His face was built of hard cheekbones, full lips, and eyes that smoldered with their brown irises. He inspected me up and down, and muttered, "Hey."

I got a good glimpse at his muscular chest, and my cock stiffened. His eyes stalked me.

I had been cruised by guys in college, and even a couple of times in the forest preserve by my parents' house growing up, but I had always shied away, scared of strangers, scared of men who killed in cruising spots, scared of myself. I had just a fraction of a second now to reconsider how many times I had walked away like a cornered rat, and I broke that loop.

When the swimmer looked at me, he saw a man with no previous history. I had a chance to forget my freakish changes, and to use this body for a new purpose.

We stood close, just a foot away from each other, dripping chlorinated water. I took my hand and cupped it around his balls. I knew how to do this by pure instinct, but I had never had a chance to act upon it.

The guy leaned in close to me, and he grabbed me by the back of the neck. "You like to fucking play, dontcha?" he said.

His grip awoke something inside of me.

I put my hand on his bulge. I squeezed harder on his nuts and kissed him on the lips for a few moments, tasting the sweetness of his mouth, and relishing those thick lips.

I ran my hands up and down his hard stomach and his thick pecs, and I squeezed on his nipples while my bulge pressed against his.

"Uh uh, none of that," he said, slapping my hands away from his chest. "We do things my way."

He grabbed my ass, cupping each muscled globe and pressing it close to him. Then, in one swift move, he pinned my arms behind my back, forcing his kisses on me. He was twisting really hard, and pain shot through me.

I was so hard I could burst. Cramps danced up my arms and shoulders, and a gentle heat spread through my chest, stomach and crotch, as the swimmer pressed his body up against me. His cock tented up his shorts.

By sheer size, I was way bigger. He was compact and muscled, probably 5'6", with legs that looked strong enough to crush a walnut between them. I had way more mass, but he had way more aggression.

The swimmer used his pin on my arms to twist me quickly, and he slammed me down on the row of sinks next to his locker. My body folded over at the waist. My ass went straight up in the air in my black Speedo. I could see my face in the mirror for a fraction of a second. I felt something in my cock move into a harder form, like a machine coming online.

I glimpsed my reflection.

My shoulder muscles flexed, the fibers beneath the skin rippling. They were monstrous shoulders made of nothing but muscle. My head went down low into the basin of the sink as the swimmer jammed it. I wanted more.

I waited for this guy's cock, but instead, he left me hanging for a moment. He grabbed my hands. He slipped a towel over them and tied my hands tight behind my back. He rummaged again behind me. I saw only the surface of the white basin in front of my eyes. I could smell old shaving cream coming up through the pipe and drain.

"I don't have a proper tool on me," the swimmer said. "but this will do. Ever use a paddle for swim drills?" he asked. I never got a chance to respond.

I felt the first strike of the plastic swim paddle smack right on my left buttock. Then a second one on my right one. My cock pressed itself onto the sink, and I could feel my breath shorten as pleasure went up my crotch with each burning strike of the hard, molded plastic.

"I knew you wanted this, little fucking bitch," he said.

Each strike of the paddle reminded me of the first man who ever put me into bondage and gave me pain: Nathan. I was relishing each paddle strike, and I was sure that my ass was turning bright red, the skin blooming, alive, the muscles beneath pumping hard and swelling.

The swimmer yanked me back up by my hair. A coil of pain shot up my shoulder blades as the towel that bound my wrists tightened up and my torso came up to a vertical position. He put one arm around me, over my neck. There I was, exposed like a fish about to be gutted. I could see myself in the mirror once more. My formerly hairless body now had a hairy chest and the beginnings of a trail going down into my shorts.

Something else had changed in the few seconds since I had started this game with the swimmer. The change was undeniable, and fear exploded in me. Something was coming over me, and my body had triggered another change.

My hair. What happened to my hair?

The hair on my head had gone dark. The blond locks were gone.

Instead, wet lines of dark brown glued themselves to my forehead.

My mouth flew open in surprise. I didn't want to control myself any longer. I was ready to put myself through this moment, because in doing so I could remember how I had been enslaved by Nathan, who was so far away from here now, but whose control extended like an invisible tether across the continent.

Fuck. Fuck. Fuck. My hair.

I could only repeat this phrase over and over, as the swimmer grabbed me by the cock and balls. His hand wasn't big enough to take my whole package in his palm. He squeezed until I felt excruciating pain in my testicles. He kissed the side of my neck for a moment. I could see he was enjoying this as much as I was. He lacked the finesse of my master Nathan, but I could feel drips of pre-cum staining my tight swimsuit.

"Love these little trunks," said the swimmer. He lowered his board shorts and his cock flew free, pressing right up against my crack, the tip of his dick pressing deep into my ass, wanting to rip through the shiny black nylon. I moaned into the hand he gagged me with.

He took hold of the waistband of my trunks, and he yanked hard, so hard that I would have fallen back onto him if it weren't for my new strength. His hands held onto the Speedo and it ripped right off my body. It was soaked. Whether it was from the pool water or my sweat, I don't know.

The swimmer took the ripped suit in both hands, which were turning blue from the tight restraints he knotted with the white towels.

"What are you doing?" I said.

My question was cut off as he yanked the black swimsuit over my face, smashing my nose up inside the trunks and bringing a deep shade of night over my vision. I could see myself through the mesh, bound and controlled by the stranger. The layer of water trapped in the weave of the nylon trunks made it hard to breathe, and I panicked a bit. The mask that it made was confining, and I took big gulps of air. They were futile. He tied the suit around my head, leaving my face encased in it. I didn't want to lose air.

I could feel his breathing touching my shoulder blades, and his hard cock slipped against the inside of my thigh.

"Fuck. No condom," he said. "We can work around that."

The swimmer took his right hand and extended his index and middle finger. He leaned me over slightly over the sink again, and he put his fingers on the edge of my asshole. "Time to make you a man," he said.

His fingers were long and thick, and he worked them up and down my sphincter. Waves of pleasure shot through me, and I gasped for air. Using his other hand, he began to jerk me off while his two fingers explored me.

His fingers found their spot, and their knuckles and ridges provided me with extra spasms inside. As he thrust in deeper, I felt him touch my prostate, and immediately I began to feel a swelling inside of the sweetest pleasure. This was an orgasm that felt long and deep, like a sunset. He pumped my cock, which was wet with pre-cum.

The pumps on my dick got faster, and when I couldn't take the pressure in my prostate, I came, long and hard, moaning into the nylon yanked over my face. Streams of my cum hit the floor of the locker room, and I moved my hips back to feel the swimmer's cock again. He yanked the trunks off my face.

I looked at the floor beneath me at my feet, and the swimmer's moans filled the locker room as he came long and hard. A pool of cum hit the tiles between my feet as he jerked off behind me.

The sound of our ragged breathing filled the space of the greasy little locker room. It was a soothing sound, and we each took deep lungfuls of oxygen as our bodies relaxed.

And then, his moans of pleasure changed. I heard him gasp, and his voice rang with fear.

My face was still trapped in the swim trunks. I couldn't see very well behind the nylon, but I could see he was moving away from me, as if I might be dangerous. He had let go of the swimsuit, and it fell off onto the sink counter. I could see.

"What the fuck is going on with you, man? You sick or something?" the swimmer said.

I was straining against the towel that bound my wrists together, and I turned toward him, squaring my hips and balancing myself on my feet again. He scooped up his gym bag and his towel. He was leaving me tied up here, for sure. He was spooked by something. Maybe someone was coming to close up the gym?

"Undo me," I said.

He just shook his head. "This is fucked up, man. YOU are fucked up."

He yanked his jeans up to his waist, grabbed his duffel bag, and ran out, keeping an eye on me the whole time as if I were a wild animal.

In my ears, I heard buzzing, like that of a million bees in a hive. In my arms, I felt pain from being pulled tight by the towel. I needed to get out of here myself, before a janitor caught me, tied up, hooded with my own briefs.

The buzzing grew louder, thrumming to a beat, like music, and I flexed my forearms and triceps as hard as I could. The knot binding my wrists was tough. I yanked my arms away as hard as I could.

I heard the towel rip, and ribbons of white cotton fell to the ground behind me. It was so easy to snap the towel apart that I wondered why it hadn't occurred to me sooner. I turned back to the mirror to learn what had spooked the swimmer off so badly.

At first I thought that what I was seeing was some sort of tattoo made with permanent marker by the guy who had just tried to fuck me. In the mirror, thick red lines spread out all over my body, outlining the muscle fibers in my chest muscles and my abs. I turned sideways, and the mirror showed me similar lines in my back.

But it wasn't a tattoo. It wasn't marker, either. These lines were actual wounds, deep as the cuts made by a butcher knife. Though they weren't bleeding, I could see right into the muscle tissue, like a sirloin on a butcher's block. I was covered in hundreds of cuts. The flesh beneath pulsed, swelling and growing.

My skin was literally coming apart as my muscles burst through.

I looked like my muscles and tendons had ripped my skin open in the throes of my sexual excitement. In the mirror I could see I had grown larger, more muscular, and the hundreds of deep lines were starting to close, to seal their seams. I had once seen a shark up close and marveled how their scales had looked like slits. The cuts all over my body were slits too, and the skin closed up. My hair looked even darker now. It was raven black.

I looked around me. No blood.

My heart was beating so fast I thought I might have a heart attack.

I gathered my clothes, yanked them on in a hurry, and walked out toward the lobby. The attendant gave me a funny look, but I pretended everything was normal. I reached the hallway that led to the street. There, against the wall, I spotted a man with dark sunglasses, messing with the vending machine. He tilted his head toward me, and smiled.

It was the man from the gas station, the one who had seen me jerk off in front of him. Seeing him made me feel worse, and I wanted to run as far from this place as I could.

I never ran so fast out of a building as I did that night. I got in my car and drove off to my apartment. The muscles on my arms bulged, thick as a lumberjack's, and they throbbed, the cuts in the skin flying open like gills on a fish. I drove in moonlight until I realized my headlights needed to be turned on. My eyes looked back at me in the rearview mirror, and I hated them. Where had my blue eyes gone? I saw only pools of tar.

Everything that was happening was medically impossible. It went against everything I knew about the human body. It felt wrong.

I was still shaking when I stopped the car in front of my apartment.

I slammed a beer from the fridge and lay back on my bed for a minute to clear my head. On the nightstand I spotted a stack of comic books. I had pulled them out of storage a few weeks ago to re-read them. They were the source of so many of my fetishes, and if it weren't for them, I would never have hooked up with Nathan. And then none of this might have happened. Those damn stories of heroes in tights, bound and gagged, fighting villains only gods could face. I had jerked off to so many of their images. But I should have looked more closely at their stories of mutants and freaks. I flipped through one for a moment, and then I tossed it behind the bed. *Fuck this.*

I turned my head toward the far end of the room.

There, on my dresser, was the book *The Golden Man: A Gay Bondage Manual.* I grabbed it by the spine and threw it as hard as I could against the wall. It shattered the plaster and landed on the floor.

There were no answers in these books. Just story after story of make-believe. Even *The Golden Man's* bizarre prophecies about a man changed by the laws of time and space were more bullshit in the heap. I was done with these books. What I wanted was reality.

My phone gave off a loud beep, and I fished it out of my pockets. It was Nathan.

What do you think about spending a weekend in LA with me? I'll make it good for you, boy, read the message.

CHAPTER 6
THE PROPHECIES

My body's metamorphosis sent me down a well of black thoughts and nihilistic images. It had always been my work that always pulled me out of the depths.

But weeks into my transformation, my work was no longer a refuge.

People were noticing I was different, and it didn't take me long to figure out that I needed to leave my job as head Nurse at Arkum Memorial Hospital.

Another hospital at the western end of Kansas City was interested in hiring me. I put in my application. I needed a fresh start, a place where a 6'3" nurse built like a war tank could make a fresh start without his past trailing behind him.

While I waited to hear the final decision on my application, I prepared at home each night for my trip to Los Angeles to meet with my master, Nathan. He had invited me to his home in the hills, and I spent each night imagining the hard discipline he would give me. I dreamt of his boots, his hard pecs, and the cruel lashes from the whippings he would serve me.

I worked, and I prepared, every single day. I repeated that process for weeks, until finally, the day of my vacation arrived.

That afternoon, I drove myself to the airport and left my car in long-term parking so no one would have to drive me to the airport and wave goodbye. I hadn't seen my friends in many weeks, afraid of what they might think of my monstrous proportions and the changes in my appearance.

I put my carry-on in the overhead bin, and I marveled at the dark hair across the back of my hands. Just six months ago, that hair had been so blond it looked white. The hands themselves were different, too. Veins crisscrossed their backs. Braids of blood, hands of power.

I wedged the bag into the compartment. It slid into the slot with a loud crack. I hoped I hadn't broken the compartment. I latched it, pretended to look for my smartphone out of my pocket, and took my seat.

My shoulders used to be narrow, but now, my arms bulged out of my t-shirt. When I sat down, my triceps rubbed against the woman in the seat next to me. She grunted and buried her face in a book.

I pulled back from my seatmate so our arms didn't touch, and I leaned toward the aisle. I flipped through a magazine, but I knew I wasn't going to read it. There were too many thoughts in my mind, like ants coming up from the anthill to dominate a tree.

The day before, during a break from my shift at the hospital, I had stepped on the scale. I now weighed close to 200 lbs. That was 45 pounds of new, rock-hard muscle on my frame that had never been there before. I had never lifted weights in my life.

Though my thoughts and memories were intact, my body no longer felt like the body I had known for 28 years. My torso, my limbs, their hands and feet, even my eyelashes were different now. They all felt new.

This new flesh had come at a price. Every few days, my skin tore open, and I would emerge from its cocoon, bigger, always bigger.

My muscle tissues were growing faster than my skin could keep up with, and my skin literally parted itself to make way for the muscle. The holes in my skin opened all over my body, from the soles of my feet all the way up my torso, and even through my forehead. For a few seconds, I could see the muscles underneath as they writhed and churned.

In all my years as a nurse, I had never seen anything like this. It terrified me, and it made me want to seek medical attention. But I wasn't stupid. I knew I should keep it secret. When I realized that these tissue changes hadn't killed me, I decided to observe them carefully. A few of those nights I even monitored my pulse and blood pressure to see how the transformation affected them. They remained normal. I began to keep a log.

I noticed that after each growth spurt, I felt agile, more alert. These feelings intensified one day after another. I began to look forward to the mornings after the changes, because each time I felt better.

So far, the changes hadn't impacted my health negatively. In fact, I was healthier and stronger than ever before.

So I waited it out. I observed. I tracked and wrote down my vitals. I logged the changes in a journal. In my notes, I named the process ripping, because I could actually hear the skin come apart like a piece of fabric while the muscles underneath ballooned up to a new size.

During these ripping episodes, I never bled, but I wished I could. Blood would mean that I could feel some emotion, but I couldn't really find one. When my skin split this way in the middle of the night while I lay in bed, I would wonder if Nathan had done this to me; all of this had started around the time I met him, when I committed myself to be his boy, his slave.

I wondered if he thought about me much. I wanted to be close to this man like no man I had ever met, but this closeness involved pain, bondage, and hard discipline. I wondered what he might think of my new body and its new muscular frame. I wanted him to love my thick back muscles and my firm ass, and I wanted him to tell me he loved me, too. But that phrase would have to come at the end of his whip, or at the tip of the electric wand he liked to put to my balls. After the handful of long sessions of pain and bondage he gave me in Kansas City when we lay in his hotel suite, he would lean in close, and he would let me mold my body around his for comfort. This was the time when we came down from the intensity of the rope, the gags, the clamps. But he never spoke words that shed light on his emotions. Never. I guess we were good friends who knew how to fuck in this dangerous and intimate way, but nothing more.

The sky looked bright through the windows. It was blue underneath it all, but the sun washed out even the clouds.

In the middle of the flight, I grew more restless. I had kept the book *The Golden Man* tucked inside my jacket during the flight. Now I pulled it out and cradled it in my palm, like a talisman.

About the book: I learned that *The Golden Man* could be read in various ways. At first glance, the book's cryptic instructions on how to tie up men showed the reader how to not fear bondage, and in fact, its words made bondage a thing of beauty and precision, a work of art to rival David and the Parthenon.

The book's author, Salvatore Argento, filled its chapters with descriptions of a perfect male body, with detailed formulas that indicated the proportions of his legs, chest, arms and even his cock, in order to mold the most perfect specimen. He derived a mathematical precision around the concept of the Golden Man, a being made of beauty itself. The Golden Man was rumored to transgress against the passage of time. He appeared in ancient times and across centuries and continents.

Argento's lavish descriptions of the Golden Man's arms, chest and legs created an image of sublime perfection. And the secret that made the Golden Man so powerful was something called the Process, an alchemical energy source that gave him his transformative power, and one which gave him the keys to the universe.

From a secondary but equally important perspective, the book told many, many stories about the Golden Man, and his many appearances over the centuries.

These stories wound upon themselves like a tangle of brambles. I read many of them over and over, trying to decipher their meaning. As my friend Joel had warned me, the book contained hundreds of stories of super human men. Some stories connected, and some stood on their own. I consumed them all. Decades ago, I had read superhero comics this way.

I read over one of the stories I had bookmarked while the plane approached LAX.

The story was a legend that Argento had collected during his research in archeological archives. The story told the legend of a man who had once lived on the shores of the Yucatan peninsula, in the days before the Spanish arrived with their horses and instruments of metal. This story took place in the days when jaguars used the speech of men. This man, according to Argento, had been chosen by the jaguars of the jungle as the perfect expression of the god of the wind. His long neck and wide shoulders could move whole boulders, and the muscles in his legs rivaled the strength and speed of the most ferocious jaguars of the tribes.

The man lived alongside the jaguars for many years, where he revealed to them his secrets. The man performed acts of sorcery in the jungle, beneath the red cities of the Maya. To protect the man and his beauty, the jaguars invented riddles that warded off the warriors from the cities who tried to find his location in the jungles. The jaguars harbored the man until one day he walked down into a sinkhole in the ground, slowly, as the crystal-clear water of the pit swallowed him whole. He never emerged from the sinkhole again. The secrets of his perfect figure and god-like face remained buried in the riddles that lived under the roars and purrs of the jaguar. It was said that the jaguars kept the man secret from the god of the wind himself, who would have broken into a rage of jealousy if he had gazed upon the human's face.

The whirling thrum of the plane's engines plucked me out of the story. We were about to land.

I was lost in these thoughts as the plane touched down at LAX. I exited the plane and collected my bag.

I walked out into the taxi stand to wait for a cab. Within an hour I would be in Nathan's territory, staying with him for a weekend. Would he pull out all the stops and put me through severe punishment? Up until now, we had only played together in his hotel rooms in Kansas City, where he came in for business meetings. What could a week with my master look like in his territory?

I walked out of the terminal and into the California air. The taxi line was long, and the sun blinded me as it spilled onto the concrete and dusk crept in. I looked over my shoulder and spotted a man in dark glasses, a black t-shirt, and jeans, waiting for a taxi with the rest of the people in line. His pecs bulged through the fabric, and tight hard nipples punctuated the rounded surface of his chest. Veins crept down his biceps and forearms, and the brown stubble on his chin glinted in the orange sunlight. His legs were taut and strong, like a gymnast before taking on the pummel horse. I spotted a huge bulge and thick-veined cock in his khakis. My own dick stirred with excitement at his sculpted body. He squatted low to the ground to rummage through his bag, and I could see the tight lines of his underwear cut across his bulging ass.

An urge came over me. I considered what it would be like to fuck this man. I didn't often think about topping a man, but this man's sculpted physique made me wonder how much my extra weight would feel pressing down on him as I pounded those two perfect ass cheeks. My cock stirred in my shorts. At Nathan's request, I hadn't jerked off in a week, and I could feel my need for sex rise inside me like a column of smoke. Under my terms with Nathan, I was at his service at all times. This meant that I was to only have sex with him, even though I may be tempted to have sex with other men. I didn't generally agree with these rules, but he had imposed them on me in the past few weeks during our phone calls, with an authoritative tone I couldn't turn down. I didn't want to lose the sexual pleasure he was bringing to me with his domination, so I accepted them, but I was always tempted, and as my body was changing, my urges also grew.

The man removed his dark glasses. His eyes were as perfect as the rest of his body. Their color was hard to define. Maybe they were amber, maybe they were green. The setting sun dusted them with yellow.

I felt dizzy all of a sudden, and I shielded my eyes from the horizon. Maybe I needed some water. The man smiled at me. I could see the soft rise and fall of his chest as he breathed in the smog of Los Angeles.

And then, I realized who this man was. My stomach coiled into a ball of fear.

I fumbled and I dropped my cell phone. I picked it up off the ground and used my fumble to get a good look at his face. This was the same man who had spotted me in the parking lot back in Kansas City on the day Nathan had given me orders to masturbate in public. He was also the same man who tipped his hat off to me after my abuse at the hands of a swimmer at the local public pool. I had lost sight of the man when I had gone back inside the gas station bathroom to change, and I had run away from him the night at the pool, but I remembered the face well. His features remained boyish, but his good looks exuded a deep masculinity.

"Wanna share a taxi?" he said. The two people in line between us shifted aside for a second, and the man got a better look at me. I forgot that I had grown taller. So many of the changes in my body were hard to keep track of.

"Sure," I said. "As long as you're headed to Santa Barbara."

"It's on my way, no worries; I'm just going part of the way."

I could have just taken a cab by myself as planned, but I was ahead of schedule, and though Nathan was waiting for me, I didn't mind taking a detour. At that moment, I felt I needed to get closer to this stranger who had followed me, to know who he was. He assured me he was going my way, as if I hadn't heard him the first time. We put our bags in the back of my taxi, and I followed his perfect back as he entered the taxi. He didn't carry more than his duffel bag. He carried it with him into the taxi. His body was packed with muscle, and his skin smelled of the woods.

I didn't hesitate for one second once we were riding in the back of the cab.

"I know you," I said. "You spotted me outside a gas station in Kansas City last summer."

The man nodded, and he glanced out the window at the concrete and glass of Los Angeles.

"You're right about that, friend. That day you came out and pumped your cock until you came. The time of day was the same as it is now. The sun was setting in front of you. I saw you at the pool, too, in the nighttime. I was glad to see you again that day, too. My name is Victor."

He put his hand out. Electricity surged into my palm as we shook hands. He bowed slightly as he did so. There was something about his gestures that felt very, very old-fashioned. It felt so formal to shake hands, and yet I appreciated the man's candor. But I had so many more questions than just what his name was.

"What are the chances you would run into me on this flight, and how do you remember me from that day? I didn't look quite the same then as I do now," I said.

"Your eyes and your hair, they are dark like night," Victor said. "But you are not a dark man. It doesn't take skill to read character from a man's face. I've been hoping to find yours again, and to see you in person up close. Each week you have been changing faster than the last. I have enjoyed observing the changes. Your beauty and your strength are powerful enough to kill."

"You have been following me," I said. It was not a question for Victor. It was a firm statement. This time, I let the deepness of my voice come at him like a ram. I didn't want to let him think I was scared of him. Though I was.

During the past months I had felt certain that someone was watching me. I would feel this sometimes when I would strip my briefs off and step into the shower, knowing that it was easy to see through the window and into the privacy of my bath. Sometimes the feeling would come over while I was driving the back roads at night, returning from a movie in the suburbs. I had the feeling there were eyes in between the houses that lined the back roads of Kansas City as I drove into my neighborhood. Quiet eyes.

There were even times in the middle of the night where I would wake up and look out my windows, wondering if there had been a person standing on the fire escape, just minutes before. Each time I stepped out to investigate, I would only find a breeze under a starry sky.

Victor's gaze drifted off into the windows again, dreamy-eyed. His profile would make any woman's heart melt and make a man go mad with envy. Despite his muscled body, he had a gentleness that I had never felt from any man before. I had certainly not felt it from Nathan, with his army general's personality and his need to discipline a submissive like me. No, Victor felt gentle and almost fragile, like the crystals in a snowflake that floated down to the floor of the woods.

"I have seen you carrying *the book*," Victor said.

"You know about *The Golden Man*?" I said.

He nodded. My copy of *The Golden Man* was one of my few prized possessions now. I couldn't solve its riddles, but the book gave me comfort.

"*The Golden Man* has been interesting, though not particularly useful. Archimedes, mathematics, alchemy, and bondage. Never thought I'd read a book quite like it," I said.

Victor put his palms together, as if he were squeezing a paper towel into a ball. For a few moments, the air around his hands shifted, and a sound like a faraway musical instrument bounced inside the back seat of the cab. The skin on Victor's hands split apart like the skin of a ripe tomato, and I saw right into his sinew and bone. Red beds of muscle and ropes of fascia strained through the knuckles, and I was reminded of my own ripping episodes. I could see the blood pumping beneath the skin. It was like X-ray vision. The skin flared open for a few seconds, and then it was gone.

He was like me.

"I once lived in the Pacific Northwest, just outside Portland. I had a wife, and two children that had moved away to other states with their own children," Victor said. "I had never told my wife I was interested in men, and she never really suspected. But I had been attracted to them since I was in high school. I lived in the closet for more than 40 years. When I was 60, I came across a copy of *The Golden Man* in the special collections wing of the university library. I too found its secret, just like you did. And the Process changed me into this. That was ten years ago."

Victor claimed to be the living embodiment of The Process, the very secret that gave power to the super human men found in the tales of the book *The Golden Man*. *I could never have imagined something as strange as this.*

I looked at his body, at how it looked like living marble. This was no man of 70 years old. It was impossible to look that virile, that young, even with the latest advances in cosmetic surgery and hormone therapy.

Well, fuck me. I've gone raving mad.

Maybe today was the day to start believing in tooth fairies and pink elephants, I thought. My own skin had split like a ripe fruit and my muscles had grown, without any steroids or manmade chemicals, into a raven-haired Atlas. My eyes, my hair, they had all become something thicker, stronger. As long as the reality of those changes was true, what would stop another man from changing also, even if the change seemed to *reverse* time? I couldn't put away my belief in science and everything I had learned in nursing school, but for a few moments, I had to lay it aside, in order to not feel a migraine coming on.

Victor's face twitched, but even that nervous tic was handsome, rugged, filled with sexual magnetism. Sure enough, there were grooves in the forehead and creases at his eyes and mouth that indicated he was a more mature man, but he didn't look a day past 40. Hell, 35 even.

"Let's say I take you at face value for a moment," I said, trying to protect myself from this stranger. For now, I had to humor him in order to learn more. He might be convincing, but I couldn't trust him. "What value is there in following me?"

"Company," Victor said. "I have been on my own for a long time. When I went through the Process, the changes to my body happened very slowly. They took many years, in fact. But what changed faster than my musculature was my mind. The changes brought on by the Process were too much to bear. My consciousness was not equipped to deal with the burden of this knowledge. Even the book couldn't help me.

"When I read *The Golden Man*, I experimented with its techniques on myself, and the changes were immediate. Any man can become the Golden Man, by hook, or by crook. I chose crook. I experimented with LSD and electroshock therapy, as well as whatever brain medications I could get my hands on to spur the changes on. With each unethical experiment on myself, with each acid trip, with each exploration of my genetic code, I got closer. Just like the book said I would.

"At that time, I was a few years away from retirement, and I was still teaching undergrads. That's when Ernie, one of my students, came into my life. I fell in love with Ernie immediately. His big ears, his crooked dick, but most of all, his company and his love. That year I began a secret affair with him; he was 40 years younger than me, young enough to be my son. He witnessed my bodily changes, my 'life in reverse,' as he used to call it. He saw me grow young.

"Every day I could see there were changes that were beyond my control. I was growing taller, stronger, more attuned to my senses. But though Ernie provided me sex, conversation, and his presence, I found that I was more alone than I had been before. You see, lies can't live for this long without poisoning those who create them. My wife knew something was wrong, but we were both good at pretending. It was easier that way. She knew about my life with Ernie, but she never got up the nerve to confront me.

"One Saturday morning, while she was at her yoga class, I left her a note in the kitchen saying I was going to the mechanic to get a tune-up for our SUV. I walked out the door dressed in a pair of jeans and a red sweater, because fall was just arriving. I never went back to that house. I walked east, determined to destroy everything I had, at all costs. That day I walked away from Ernie too. I left the state without telling him what I was doing. I don't know what ever became of him."

We rode in silence for about a minute, and I still felt fear tightening up my throat. Anxiety was pricking my insides. Victor's chiseled handsomeness literally glowed in the afternoon sun. I also felt sorry for him.

"It's funny," I said, "the changes I have gone through… Some of them have made me lonely, but I haven't experienced it the same way you have. I am sorry you have felt this way."

I wasn't sure why I was saying this to Victor, but it was true. He looked lonely. His eyes were empty, and his hulking body, though impressive, lacked a certain vigor. I had seen injured animals and terminally ill patients look the same before, moments before going under the scalpel of a surgeon.

"That's why I went out to find you," Victor said. "There was a rumor that there might be another Golden Man out there. A person who was harnessing the Process. So I set out to look for him. And I found him. I found you.

"I want to show you what the Process can do, but also, I want to be with you, to know you are real. To touch skin that rips away from the muscles like mine does. I want to know that someone out there understands this metamorphosis I am always living in."

Victor laid his right hand on my pec, and I felt heat transfer to me. He leaned over and kissed me, and I let him. There was no pity on my part. I was simply curious to know what it was like to kiss someone who had changed, just like I had changed.

He tasted like wet earth after a storm. My prick hardened under my jeans, and I felt him tense up under his polo shirt. I kissed back harder. My hands fell onto his waist and then his bulge. I felt a thick rod, tight against his trousers, and beneath, a round package of firm testicles. I kissed his neck, cradled his shoulders. From the corner of my eye, I spotted the cab driver, who put his sunglasses on and turned up the radio.

I was not prepared for the incredible hardness of Victor's flesh. His muscles were so dense, I felt like he was made of poured concrete. Was my own body like this? I didn't think so. He felt heavy, and his abs were ripped under his shirt. Grooves of granite. As he shifted in the seat, I could hear some of the seams ripping on his pant leg. As he flexed, his leg muscles burst through the khaki fabric.

He looked me straight in the eye, and I felt a trance, like time stopping for a moment. I remembered drowsy days in winter in Kansas. They were days that were short, low on light. I had stayed under the blankets a little extra those mornings. The snow covering the city had made me sad, and the gray sky above had dusted the air with shadow. Victor's eyes were exactly like those winter days. His brown hair was thick, a young man's mane. There wasn't even a single gray hair on it.

I unzipped my jeans, and my cock sprang up as my lower back tightened up, arching, and my chest heaved up and down as I breathed in the stale air of the taxi, which smelled of old cigarette smoke and sweat. Victor worked his mouth up and down my shaft, caressing the pattern of veins and curling his tongue around my head, which glistened. The back of his head lay beneath me, and I ran my hands through the auburn waves. I put my hand on top of it and pushed him down on my cock. He obeyed and my penis hit the back of his throat. His tongue on my skin made me moan, and the cab driver cocked his head after he heard me. This felt like when I had jerked off at the gas station: exposed, public, vulnerable, and yet not. I had never seen a body as perfect as Victor's, and even Nathan's rock-hard body didn't seem to flow into its proportions the way Victor's did now.

Victor grabbed my balls through the denim of my jeans, and with his free hand he ran his hand up the back of my shirt. Every inch of my skin took in his touch like a computer gathering a large set of data. His hands were smooth, and they ran up my lat muscles. Since I had begun transforming, I had spotted small black hairs sprouting there, and these thin hairs came alive now, giving my sense of touch and extra dimension, like an extra sense. Victor's throat caressed my cock. I was close to cumming.

I wanted to rip Victor's shirt off, to dig my fingers into his pecs and make him hurt, and I wanted him to groan with pleasure. I wanted to dominate this perfect specimen. If I could, I'd have yanked his tight briefs down from his bubble ass and tried to fuck him with my cock. This image was bright and real, a wonderful daydream while we rode in the cab.

What I was doing right now violated Nathan's rules over me, but I didn't care. I felt something inside of me pushing faster than my brain could keep up with.

I felt Victor's dick throb under the pressure of my hand on his khakis, and I could see he had stained his khakis with pre-cum. He pumped my cock with his hand as he slathered his spit and worked up my tool. He licked me up and down, and teased my head with his sensuous lips. Pressure swelled inside me, and my cock felt like it was going to burst.

Then I heard a snap in the back of my neck, and a wave of pleasure surged through me. I came in thick spurts of cum into the man's mouth, marveling at the wetness and warmth. Victor swallowed every ounce of my seed, and electric shocks surged through my body, up and down, up and down, as the orgasm blew open my insides. Loads of my milk went down his throat, and he swallowed again with joy. My vision went dark for a moment, and I saw a symbol, a circle of bright light, intersected by a single straight line. I was having a vision again. My balls tightened up, and I came for a third time, as another orgasm delivered an aftershock to my system.

I could smell the cigarettes that had been smoked in this cab over the years. They became layers and layers of past smokes, etched into the leather interiors. I also smelled the ghosts of perfume, sweat and aftershave of previous riders. These exploding scents blew up in my brain. Now I detected the smell of my sweat, Victor's sweat, and the air freshener hanging from the dashboard that carried with it traces of the Chinese factory where it had been manufactured. I smelled diesel and human waste from the streets outside as the LA air crept through us via the window.

Victor came up for air, and sweat beaded little stars on his forehead. His sullen eyes changed, and he cracked a single smile up at me.

"They're following us," he said. "The book said someone will follow us, and it's all coming true. You see, the book is filled with riddles and mathematical theorems, but it's also filled with prophecies."

"Who's following us?" I asked. He pressed the palm of his hands on his thick bulge, as if it could make his erection fade. It couldn't. The busted seams in the sides of his trousers near the thighs and his calves revealed his pale skin beneath. His chest was swelling, too, like a cobra preparing for attack. He was panting now. He looked out the window, glancing at the other cars on the street. We were crossing downtown LA now. He looked scared.

"Damn that book," Victor said. "The sky is so dark now, and all I can do is follow that book. It has taken over my life." Smog tinged the sky gray, but otherwise, the sun shone bright and clear. There were no clouds. The sparseness of the sky filled me with dread.

He zipped me up, gave me another kiss deep inside my mouth, and stood straight in his seat, his submissive pose gone. "Thank you, sir," he said.

No one had ever called me sir in a context of sex. I felt in awe. I put my hand back on his shoulder. What I touched was no longer flesh. It was solid and dense like a precious metal. Like a slab of silver or an ingot of titanium.

We turned a corner, and the look of worry on Victor's face darkened even further. He glanced out the back window again and grunted.

He gave me another long glance, his eyes reaching out toward me. Pleading.

And then, as the car moved through the street, Victor grabbed his black bag, pulled the door handle on his left, and he yanked the door open. He jumped out into the street, and he rolled sideways and out. He hit a newspaper box hard with his head, and he sent it flying over. Under normal circumstances, he should have died on the spot. But he bounced off in one piece. It was the box that didn't make it. It collapsed like a tin can.

The cab driver hit the brakes, and we speeded to a halt at the stoplight.

Victor tumbled, landed in front of a sandwich shop, and he stopped rolling just short of the glass window. He was still clutching his bag. He stood up immediately and looked both ways, to see who had seen his crash.

From where I was, I could tell that the newspaper box hadn't even put a scratch on him. I moved closer to the open door of the cab to go help him. I was familiar with car trauma injuries and knew I could help him while we waited for an ambulance.

I hadn't even put out one of my legs from the cab when I saw that Victor was fully recovered and standing on both feet. He catapulted into a full run, as if his heels were spring-loaded. He ran faster than I had ever seen a human being run. He took off down the street, looking back over his shoulder once to look me in the eyes. I knew that look in his gray eyes: *Don't follow me, kid.*

I was due at Nathan's apartment in minutes, and I hadn't even texted him yet to say I had arrived in L.A. If Victor was truly like me, I knew that his wounds would be minimal. And that's if he had any wounds at all. I myself had found that sharp objects and blunt trauma did little to my muscles and bones nowadays.

The book said someone will follow us, and it's all coming true, Victor had said. I shut the door to the cab. The driver took his sunglasses off and turned over the seat to look me straight in the eyes.

"Listen, faggot," he said. "You know you're going to have to pay me in cash, right? I don't care what kind of Olympic-runner steroid fuck game you're running, you *better* have my money. And you better forget this cab and permit number, capisce?"

I nodded.

"Capisce."

I wanted to laugh, because suddenly all of this was very funny. It was ridiculous, in fact. *I am seriously losing my grip on reality. Time for the straitjacket, except I might get a hard-on from wearing it.* I laughed out loud. But the cabbie did not look amused. He turned around and continued driving. We were headed to Nathan's apartment, and I was going to keep this incident a secret for now. I couldn't really trust Victor, but I wasn't ready to tell Nathan about it, either. I inspected my jeans for signs of my cum, but I saw that Victor had licked everything clean. The peaks and creases in my jeans' bulge looked like nothing had ever happened.

Victor had called me sir.

I turned the word *sir* over and over in my mind.

CHAPTER 7
ENSLAVEMENT

I spent three nights in Nathan's apartment. His home was a towering pyramid made of glass, brushed steel, and white walls, and it crested the top of a cliff, exposed like a monument, but also insular, a fortress full of secrets. "I call this place the White Pyramid," Nathan said.

The first night, he led me into his living room, a sparse room flooded by the light coming through its glass walls. He embraced me for a long time, and I wondered when our game of bondage might begin. He had never greeted me this way, but this was his home. My heart rose in my throat, because this was what I had been waiting for — a closer connection to Nathan, a connection mediated by the coils of rope and the paddles he put to my skin. He kissed me on the lips, for an endless amount of time. "You look so strong now," he said. "You have gone from David to Goliath in just a matter of weeks. You said you are doing this without drugs?" he said. I nodded. "No drugs," I said. "I can't stop the changes."

He ran his hand down my hairy chest, and up and down my meat-packed biceps. His erection sprang in his linen trousers, and he smiled up at me. I had grown taller than him, and I had to get used to the new perspective. He was still built like a muscled athlete, and his shoulders and upper back tapered down to his taut stomach, his tight little waist, his muscled ass, and legs that filled out his white trousers.

I had brought secrets with me to Nathan's white palace, and I was a man who believed in honesty, at least most of the time. I wanted our weekend together to be perfect, and I decided to level with him. It was time to deliver these secrets and render them open.

"I have a confession to make," I said. Nathan listened. I told him how the swimmer in the locker room back in Kansas had tied my hands and rammed my hole, and how I let a man suck me off outside the airport. I did

66

not explain that the man had been following me, and I avoided any details about the book *The Golden Man,* which I stowed away in the inside pocket of my suitcase. Nathan took in the news with his chin tucked, his hands in his pockets.

I had broken Nathan's rules, and the confession gave me a touch of relief.

When I confessed, a smile parted Nathan's lips, and satisfaction warmed his cheeks. "You have been wanting to test me, boy," he said. I nodded. I had to admit he was right. I knew these adventures might meet his disapproval, and now here I was, vulnerable but bathed in truth.

"Boys break rules," Nathan said. "Boys break rules." Then he shouted it a third time. "Boys break rules.

"And that's how we're going to punish you, then," he said. "Strip," he said, and I did as he asked. He stripped down to a white jock, and his bronzed Mediterranean skin glowed with sweat, even under the air-conditioned air of his palace. I got on my knees, and he inspected me. He walked around me in circles, evaluating my quads, calves, and arms.

When he got to my ass, Nathan spanked me with his hand a hundred times until the skin burned like battery acid. I know he hit me one hundred times, because he made me count each strike out loud. When he was done, he grabbed a Speedo from my bag. He didn't have to ask what I had packed; he knew I only brought the fetish gear that got me hard.

He ordered me to wear it. I slipped the swim trunks over my gigantic legs and then my ass. I tucked my bulge into the stretchy nylon. We then walked to the bathroom, where he pushed me over the edge of the sink. He bound my hands with rope, white rope, and he tied it tighter than usual so that it bit into my skin. This time, he didn't care if it burned; he was bent on punishing my transgressions. He took a red ball gag and stuffed it deep in my mouth. I could see his bulging pecs in the mirror, and he promised me that whores in swimming pools got what they deserved. He was making me re-live the night with the swimmer as punishment. He put on a condom and he fucked me deep and without lube, to show me he was boss. My ass burned as his dick went inside me, and his girth felt good and painful at the same time. When I slid forward toward the mirror, his right hand shot out and cupped its palm around my mouth and nose, and for a few minutes I got no air while he pounded my ass. He came explosively, and he remained hard even as he took off the condom.

Then, he grabbed my wrists, using the rope as a makeshift handle, and he brought me over to his living room. He sat me next to him, and I grunted into my ball gag. He slapped my face, and he crushed my chin with his hand. "You happy to cheat on me, boy? Happy to break the rules? You're going to show me how you sucked off that cocksucker at the airport."

You don't know that he was the one sucking me off, master. And I'm not going to tell you, because it felt so good to be in charge, to push his head down on my cock.

Nathan looked me in the eyes, and then he yanked me by the neck onto his jock. I struggled for air as my mouth slid onto the white cotton, and the saliva flowing around the ball gag spilled onto his bulge. He undid the straps on the gag and he set it gently on the table, perfectly lined up on the glass the way a surgeon might lay down an instrument. With my mouth free to suck his cock, he pushed me down on his rod, and I blew him for what seemed like hours. He pumped his hips up and down, and he kissed the back of my head. When he came, he spurted multiple loads, most of them in my mouth, the last one splashing on my forehead, nose, and lips. Rivers of ivory ran down my nose and onto my chin. I found this torture, and the resulting ache in my throat and the cramps in my jaw, delicious.

Afterward, he stuffed me with a butt plug, and he left me with my hands bound on his bed. He pulled the Speedo back over my ass and cock after he plugged me, and he patted the base every few minutes to drive the thick silicone rod inside. He put the ball gag back in my mouth, and I lay there all night, waiting to service him again. He slept with me, but he stayed silent, to show me the extent of his discipline and disapproval.

On the second day, Nathan undid my ties, and he let me stretch out and piss. My bladder was burning. Then we spent some time eating breakfast outside at the swimming pool. Nathan didn't ask me much about my real life back in Kansas, but he was gentle. His voice was calm, and he smiled under the warmth of the sun. I was plugged the whole time.

He brought me a change of swim trunks in the afternoon. At that time, he removed the plug and let my ass get a break. Later, he served me a lunch of sashimi and salad, which I ate with relish. I understood that our relationship was built on my sexual servitude, but he didn't want to go full-time with it. After all, who could remain tied and bound for 72 hours in a row? He was smart and careful. Even if we weren't playing with pain all day, he kept his distance. This way, when he came close with the crop, his mind would be clear and ready to control my mind and body.

That afternoon, we used a room in the higher floors of the White Pyramid, overlooking the hills as the dungeon. There, Nathan tied me to a St. Andrew's cross, naked. He flogged my legs. My ass. He flogged my back. With each lash, I heard his breath, because it was hard work for him, too. He got close to breaking skin, but the pain he inflicted felt worse than a bloody wound. As the leather landed on my body, my dick hardened with pleasure, but it was impossible to fill out to its length, because Nathan had stuffed it into a chastity device, securing it with a titanium lock.

My cock throbbed with frustration, even as the flogging brought me to new heights. I felt dizzy and of clear mind, both at the same time. After he flogged me, Nathan came up close and pressed his body on mine, and I screamed with pain as my reddened skin reacted with his bronzed body. This pain was like nothing I had ever endured, and I worried that my body might split open like it had done before, but it didn't.

Nathan took me down from the cross, and then he stuffed me into a neoprene wetsuit. My cock got harder, because it reminded me of superhero costumes. And yet, the chastity device kept my thick dick suppressed. He kissed me on the lips for a long time while I stood with my arms at my side, submissive. The sun was setting, and Nathan became nothing but a shadow, with light creeping around his silhouette like an eclipse. My skin felt like hot lava from the flogging, and I was thirsty. "Please sir, water, sir," I said. Nathan nodded, said, "Yes, good boy," and he brought me two glasses of iced water. Tears ran down my face as I drank them. He never broke eye contact with me while he performed this act of kindness.

When I finished the water, the punishment resumed.

He put me into a hog-tie using black rope this time, and he left me there, on the marble floor, facedown, for what seemed like hours. He was dressed in a leather cop uniform, and he snipped the tip off a Cuban cigar. He used me as a footstool while he smoked and drank scotch. I squirmed under the ropes, and my legs cramped. I drenched the inside of the wetsuit with my own sweat. I moaned. But my complaints were futile—he had duct-taped my mouth shut with a length of tape that wrapped several times around my head. Ash fell on my shoulders, and the clouds of California rolled at the edges of my vision.

I lost track of time, but sometime in the middle of the night, Nathan undid my ties, and he placed me gently on his bed. With my legs spread wide, he fucked me for an hour, slow and steady, finding a grinding rhythm with his hips. He caressed my chest hair and punched my pecs. He kissed me sometimes, and called me a fucking cunt. Then he slapped me, and kissed me again, calling me his special boy. His dick felt so good inside me. Deep, probing my prostate, making me want to cum with every thrust.

I felt no pain, but I did feel his thick dick inside me, and I was ready to cum. He removed the chastity device and pumped my cock a little more with his hand, and I moaned into the air. I wanted to cum so badly.

Since he had let me in the door to his house, I hadn't come yet. When he brought me close to climax, he laughed, and he put the chastity device back on my dick. I screamed and screamed, begging for him to let me cum, but instead he grabbed a penis gag made of black rubber and popped it into my mouth to shut me up. He wrapped it around my head and fastened the clasp. He secured the back with another platinum lock, and he finished fucking me. I moaned into my gag, trying to yell out his name, to beg him to let me cum, to provide me with just a few moments of release. He came long and hard, and the vascularity of his chest and arms swelled his muscles up.

That night I slept curled around him, my dick imprisoned and my mouth gagged. As usual, I dreamt of nothing.

On the third day, I awoke freed from my bonds. I searched for Nathan, but I only found empty rooms. In the kitchen, I found a note from Nathan explaining that he would be back at dusk, and he expected to find me fully showered, my ass cleaned for play, and my mouth and ass prepped for him to take over. The cage around my cock was locked shut. Nathan would only allow me to cum when he was ready for me to do so. I knew I could easily snap off the chastity belt with the strength of my bare fingers, but I got extremely aroused knowing it was Nathan controlling it, controlling my dick, controlling me.

I spent the day swimming in his pool again, and I took a hike in the trail that ran up behind the property. In these moments alone, looking over the hills, I considered how tightly bound I was to Nathan. I might be free to explore his house, but I knew that I couldn't and didn't want to escape the property.

In the late afternoon, I showered and cleaned myself, as instructed. When I stepped out of the bath, my chest caught my attention. I faced the mirror and noticed that my pecs looked thicker, more muscled than before, the muscle's serrations cut like hard marble. At first glance, I thought I looked more defined than the night before. My legs had become tree trunks, rising from bulging calf to quadriceps and hamstring, and culminating in two round globes of ass muscle. The transformation had turned my rear into a bubble butt, two curves that melded perfectly with the muscles of my lower back. My pubic hair had changed too, from its previous golden color to ebony. My lack of body fat highlighted every line of muscle in a play of shadow and light.

I walked over to Nathan's bed in a white terrycloth bathrobe, and I lay down for a moment as the setting sun whitewashed the room. Dusk was arriving, and he would be here soon. My eyes grew heavy, and I drifted off into the dark hole of sleep. I am not sure how long I slept.

I awoke from the dark suddenly, and I felt a burning tug at the top of my head. My eyes flew open as I realized Nathan was yanking me by the hair up and out of the bed. He wrestled me on the carpeted floor, and I struggled back. I knew he wanted me to fight back as a slave, and I complied. He hated lazy slaves who lay limp beneath his hand.

Nathan sat on my face and forced me to suck him off while he punched my arms. We tumbled on the carpet, in the hallway, and in the bathroom. He put me in a sleeper hold and my dick sprang up, hard and flopping around as he twisted me like a hunter wrestling an alligator. He punched my pecs and slapped my balls so hard that I felt pain creep up my belly. With each strike to my dick and balls, I got harder and my breath raced further.

This muscled body that I carried — it was his to destroy. We wrestled and panted.

By the time he won the wrestling match, he had me pinned under his feet while he stood above me. He reached into his dresser and pulled out a needle, filled with a translucent amber liquid. The needle was just like the one he had used on me the night he fucked me in his hotel room. I felt danger, and a chill went up my spine when I saw the first bead of liquid arrive at the steel tip. The night in room 808 back in the hotel in Kansas City had been one of the hottest nights of my life, but the injection had felt wrong. As a nurse, I didn't feel comfortable with unknown substances going into my bloodstream. In all my years as a medical practitioner, I knew one should not let anyone inject unknown substances into one's bloodstream. Nathan moved closer.

"No," I said. I raised my arms, ready to knock Nathan off his feet.

If I were to swipe at his knee, I'd knock him over into the dresser, I thought. *Be careful not to hurt him with this new strength. Control yourself, be precise.*

I had superhuman strength, but Nathan had something I didn't: The will to control me. As my hands came up to knock him off his feet, he caught my meaty wrist in the palm of his hand. He looked me straight in his eyes, and his sweat ran off in rivulets onto my nose. "Not so quick, you fucker. You're not getting off that easy," he said. His eyes stayed connected to mine, staring right into me. I felt his control in that gaze, and my ass tightened up, craving his cock inside me again. While my thoughts drifted and my arousal distracted, he took the opportunity to make a move. He jabbed the needle right in the side of my neck and pushed the plunger.

A red-hot burn sprang in my neck, and it started to move through my arm, and then my chest, and onto my other arm. Finally, I felt the fiery sting in my legs, in every inch of my body. It was like a fever that only got hotter. My head spun.

I saw Nathan's perfect body and his stubbled face fade away in waves as the chemical took me out.

I awoke after what seemed like hours. At first, I felt relaxed, even peaceful. I tried moving to turn myself over. My legs and my arms didn't budge one inch. I tried using my abdominal muscles to sit up, but something pinned me back. I felt a sheath compress each and every one of my muscles. I used my neck to glance down at my body as best I could.

I was covered in a tight layer of blue and black spandex, all the way from my feet to my hands and up to my neck. My mouth was taped shut, and I was laid out on a slab of stone like a surgeon's table. I could see the St. Andrew's cross behind Nathan, who stood in stark contrast to the white walls of the room. He was dressed in the tightest black leather pants and shirt I had ever seen. It contoured his thick arms, his firm chest, and his narrow waist. The thickness of his dick bulged in the leather. He wore calfskin leather gloves that ended at the wrist and created a perfect seal of tight, supple leather. He looked displeased.

"I took you out, like good slaves get taken out," he said, "but you showed me just how much you need punishment. I told you to not touch yourself while I was gone today, and you broke off the cock cage. You've fucking pissed me off, boy," he said.

I shook my head. I knew I had not tampered with the chastity device, and when I lay down on the bed I remembered it had been locked and pressed under me, intact and secure. What was he talking about?

Nathan pulled out the clear cock cage from his back pocket. The device had cracked into three or four pieces of titanium and acrylic. The casing that housed the cock was sheared clear across. When I saw it, I knew what had happened. My cock had grown while I slept, cracking open the cage like an eggshell. I glanced down at myself in the black and blue spandex suit, and I saw my dick underneath the nylon at an angle, thick and veined, a new cock, and certainly not the cock I had been born with. It looked longer than it had before. In this bodysuit, I was finally dressed up like a superhero, bound against my will. I wanted to tell Nathan that it hadn't been my fault, and that I had followed his orders, but all I could do was emit muffled sounds through the black duct tape, which was wrapped several times around my head. I tasted something thick in my mouth. He had stuffed a piece of cloth in it before applying the tape. Thick leather restraints kept me pinned to the table.

"Your superhero fantasies are a crock of shit, you fucking whore," Nathan said. "You wanted to be humiliated as a little superhero? We're going to give you that and more tonight," he said. It was true, I had creamed myself so many times while looking at comic book panels like this one, with a muscle beast superhero tied by a villain. But Nathan was no villain, he was my dominant, my keeper, my master, and he cared so much about me. This was maybe even better than a supervillain threatening my life.

"I put you in your superhero suit to humiliate you a little further, you fuck." Nathan pinched my nipples and attached clamps to them. He pulled down the crotch zipper on the suit and bound up my balls with thin rope, then he attached an electro machine to the tip of my cock. While he had my crotch and ass exposed, he took a blue butt plug and slid it way up my ass. It was much wider than any plug I had ever taken in. I let out heavy moans into my gag as the silicone column slid into me, and Nathan spat on my face.

"Fucking superhero, more like a fucking superloser," he said. He zipped up the bodysuit again and slid a pair of matching blue trunks onto my muscled ass. The spandex stretched, twisted and snapped into place, molding itself around my muscled body. He turned up the dial on the electro machine , and the vibrations swept up my cock and buzzed into my cum-filled balls. I still hadn't come once during my three days in captivity in this white pyramid, and I wanted to release my semen.

But only Nathan could make that happen. My eyes rolled into the back of my head as I fell into a deep electric numbness. Each pulse of the machine brought me to new heights of pleasure, but it also felt like an army of ants crawling on my skin. The torture was unbearable.

And then he turned it all the way up to ten.

Nathan left me plugged, gagged, and electrified for twenty minutes, which to me felt like two hours. He dug in a drawer and pulled out a black object, soft and shiny-looking. It was the mask I had seen him wear the night he first fucked me in his hotel room: A hood, a mask, a liquid prison for a face.

For so many years I had envied superheroes and their face coverings, their masks of a perfect material that spandex couldn't even mimic. And here it was, a smooth black covering that matched my superhero suit of black and blue.

"This is a one-of-a-kind mask," Nathan said. "We use it to control and to discipline. And you're going to learn now not to violate the rules of your slavery. We use our chemical controls in conjunction with a tight mask to keep superhumans in their place. After this, you will never break another cock cage, boy." He slid the tight mask over my head, and it compressed my head and conformed to the contours of my face. As it slid onto my nose and lips, I felt my dick throb and my balls tighten. My fantasies of superhumans in bondage were finally a reality.

The mask blocked out most of my vision, though I could still see a few shadows and shapes, like a perpetual twilight. Nathan put his lips on mine and he kissed me through the mask. "And now begins the beatdown," he said. He released the wrist and ankle restraints, and he helped me sit up. He removed the wire that connected my cock to the electro machine, but my cock remained bound in rope, my ass plugged deep in blue silicone.

"And this is how we humiliate a superhero," he said, giving me a big shove off the table. I landed on the floor on my stomach, and the wind got knocked out of me. Before I could get up, Nathan kicked me in the ass and punched my gut. I wasn't quick enough to block the blows. He smacked my face and I felt hot stings under the mask. He grabbed me by the cock and balls, and I screamed. "Stop," I said. He let go, wound up his arms, and punched me so hard in the dick that I keeled over. My insides twisted in pain. He kicked me in the lower back hard, and I lay out sprawled, facedown on the ground.

"Fucking superheroes, little showoffs like you, do-gooders trying to show off their asses and bulges, their tight little muscles," Nathan said. I meant to get up, but as I got to my knees I heard a crack like thunder, and then a hot lash across my back. And then another, and then another, sideways, each time ripping up my back as if making an X. Nathan was whipping me, and it hurt. It hurt bad. I could hear him breathe heavily from the physical effort, and each time I tried to get up, another lash brought me down to my knees. Lines of pain ran from my back muscles all the way down to my toes and fingertips. Pre-cum was spilling from my cock onto the blue and black spandex, and I marred the perfect smooth surface of the superhero costume.

A buzzing grew in my ears, and I knew something was wrong. I could feel myself pulsating under the suit, and I knew that one of my transformations was coming on. The bodysuit stretched against my thick bulge, my thick biceps, even my calves, as my body threatened to swell like a balloon. I felt a couple of the seams pop in the thighs as my hamstrings and quadriceps grew in size.

My tits felt heavy and wet, and I could feel them straining against the bodysuit. It occurred to me that I may be wrong about the seams popping on the costume. Maybe they weren't seams coming undone. Maybe it was my skin that was ripping open beneath.

I knew that if I was bursting out of my skin, I wouldn't bleed; I never did when this happened, but the feeling inside of changing would sweep over me. Nathan's lashes, and the hard punches that he delivered to my glutes made the change faster, more intense.

Nathan grabbed me by the neck and brought me to a standing position. He shoved me forward toward the windows, and the city and the mountains loomed in my vision as we came closer to the edge. Los Angeles lay before us like a kingdom of smog, grime, glamor, and lights. The window started from the floor and ended at the ceiling, and though there were no buildings blocking our view, no neighbors to spy on us, the glass exposed us to the world.

Nathan wrapped his arm around me in a choke hold, and his dick pressed against the spandex that covered my ass. With his free hand he jammed the plug further in my ass. Bolts of pleasure ran up through my belly and chest, and warmed my insides. The lashes had cut the skin on my back, and pain flared on its skin, searing me.

He slammed me up against the thick glass. It was strong enough to take the impact of my mass, but it vibrated as all 200 pounds of me struck it. He pulled back on the choke hold and tightened his grip. Breathing became difficult.

"Your superhero fetish, your dirty little fetish, it's here for the world to see," Nathan said. "I'm going to be the one to expose you, hero." Nathan pressed my body against the glass and through the shadowy membrane of the mask I saw the drift of cars on the highway, and the shapes of houses. Their lights glittered.

Nathan breathed next to my cheek. "We may be far from the ground, but they can see you down there," he said. His voice filled my ears, and my dick tightened. "They all see you.

"What would they do if they learned this little pervert likes to get tied up in a game of cops and robbers with super suits?" he said. He lifted the bottom of the mask, exposing my chin. "What if they could all see you?"

I knew this part by heart, because all the comics I had read as a kid always had a scene where the villain threatened to unmask our hero. I was so turned on my dick felt on fire.

"What if I told you my neighbors are watching us right now, watching me defile you through this giant window?"

"No," I screamed, "no," I didn't want anyone to see this, to see me, to know of this identity. But I could only press my tongue against the black duct tape that sealed my lips. The mask felt secure and safe now, and I wanted him to keep me hooded. My dick slid on the glass, hard and full of frustrations. My ears screamed as the high-pitched tone expanded. Under the superhero costume, my muscles grew bigger, the skin splitting itself over and over, my body thickening, expanding horizontally and vertically. I was scared, aroused, and helpless.

Nathan laughed, and with one swift move, he yanked the tight black mask from my head. That single moment of unmasking had been one of my favorite sexual fantasies, and I had spilled much cum into my sheets over the years, dreaming of heroes like The Fighter, and Aracniss, unmasked.

Now it was my turn, but I didn't want it; I wanted the mask to stay on. It was safer to stay inside the hood. And Nathan had exposed me, stripping me of its comfort. The mask flew off, and I breathed in fresh air, struggling to get free from his grip. The lights below in the valley terrified me. They were floating in a sea of darkness. In a sea of nothing.

Despite my new muscularity, Nathan's years of hard work in the gym made him a solid match for me. My black hair was matted to my forehead, and his arm coiled around my neck like a noose.

"They can all see you now, little hero. You're fucking done," he said. I screamed under the tape and felt my dick turn to steel in frustrated arousal.

Nathan released me from his grip and breathed in silence for a moment, still laughing to himself at my humiliation. He then took ultimate control. With my body encased in that tight black spandex suit, he yanked the blue trunks down my thighs. He undid the ass zipper and let my throbbing cock press against the glass. He then yanked on the crotch and pulled backward hard, giving me a painful wedgie that cut into my balls but also sent the butt plug deeper into my crack. He grabbed its base and he pulled out the silicone missile, all the while guiding my hands to press their palms against the glass. "Do not move these hands, fucker," he said.

A few moments of stillness passed, and I tried catching my breath. A hard object interrupted the calm. Nathan's dick was now at the tip of my ass, on the very pink rosebud of my ass. He pushed in with force, and I felt his welcome girth go in, while under the tape I wanted to say, *thank you, master.*

Nathan fucked me hard, sliding his large cock inside me, and grinding up and down, while I sweated into my bodysuit. The gag stayed on, but he cupped his hand over my nose and jaw occasionally, to show me he was in control. His dick was warm and a welcome change to the silicone of the plug. While he fucked me, I was growing, changing, and I could even feel the muscles in my neck tense and relax as they grew into a new shape.

I remembered Victor in the taxi, and his words. His body had been as hard as a war tank. *They're following us,* he had said. And the dark hills and the pinpoints of light below offered no relief. I felt eyes roving over me, looking up at the two muscled men in the pyramid of white steel and glass, fucking. Something or someone watched over us. I was prey.

Nathan's hips came in hard and fast, and then they moved into a smoother, slower rhythm, and he kissed my neck, like the master that he was. I did as I was told, and though I knew I had not broken the chastity device that he put on me during this weekend, I felt sorry for violating Nathan's rules. "Sorry, master," I mumbled into my gag, and his dick moved in deeper.

Sorry, master. Sorry.

My breath raced. I felt his wide chest caress my back. He came inside of me, and my sensitive hole felt his hot semen fill the latex condom one, two, three times over. He kept on thrusting even as he reached orgasm, and he put his arm around my throat again as he pumped me and his body came down into a new state of relaxation. I shut my eyes, and behind my eyelids, I saw shapes of bright light fill the darkness. I saw a symbol in those shapes, a circle bisected by a vertical line. The symbol of the Process. I didn't need the book to explain it to me; I knew it as if it were pure instinct. The golden symbol hung in the air for a few seconds, and then it faded. I opened my eyes again and Nathan was there, two inches away from me.

"The next time we meet, I will let you come. This time, we will consider this visit 100 percent training. You may suck my cock tonight and tomorrow, but you will only be allowed to cum when you arrive back in Kansas City. You will need to think about all the ways you broke the rules."

I nodded, unable to speak through the duct tape.

Nathan brought me over to his bath, and he lathered me in the shower, careful to not irritate the deep lashes on my skin from the whip. My skin had sealed up again, but I could feel how my body had grown. My traps felt thicker, my neck solid with new muscle. He inspected my abrasions and put disinfectant on them. That night he curled himself around me, and I lay in his bed, clean, safe, and sound, with my cock locked in a new cage. I knew I had probably grown by an inch or two in the heat of the scene, but I kept my observations to myself.

But Nathan was too smart. He caught me looking in the mirror, and he smirked. He cackled. He was laughing at me.

"You can't hide your transformation from me, boy," he said. He put an arm around his belly to contain his laughter.

"I know you have grown again, he said. You've grown a lot. Be sure to keep it secret. It's safe information that I will help you keep. You wouldn't want to become a media sensation," he said. The bed under us was a paradise of softness and the scent of cedar. Nathan's olive skin glinted under the moonlight that spilled into the room. I drifted off into sleep.

"Silence is better," he said. He put a finger to my lips as I shut my eyes for the night.

The next day I rose at dawn and called a taxi to take me back to the airport. Nathan felt no more real than before. We ate breakfast in silence, and I took one last swim in his pool. My Speedo barely contained my newly transformed ass cheeks. The water enveloped my skin with a velvet touch, and I relished each breath as I stroked. I emerged from the pool, towering over Nathan, and he gave me a last kiss. I had so many questions about the night before, and I wanted to demand an explanation about the injection, but I panicked. By protesting about the needle, I might lose all of this sexual pleasure. I would possibly lose Nathan if his anger took over. I decided to keep my mouth shut. Twenty minutes later, a taxi pulled up to the driveway, and I was on my way back to Kansas City.

Nathan's cruelty and his discipline felt real, and the marks he left on my body were real, but I boarded the plane that morning still not sure of how real Nathan's heart might be.

CHAPTER 8
THE CANYON AT THE END OF THE WORLD

Excerpt from *The Golden Man: A Gay Bondage Manual*, by Salvatore Argento, 1898.

The Golden Man has manifested his presence in the universe in various forms across the structures of time. The phenomenon of the Golden Man appears in the earliest forms of civilization, starting with the Phoenicians and continuing through the late 18th century. In the 19th century the legend fades away from public consciousness. What is consistent throughout this tenure is the notion of the Golden Man's relationship with concepts of chaos and destruction.

Over the span of recorded history, the Golden Man has assumed several names.

Arcane oral histories in the Nordic tradition regarded him as a human embodiment of Ragnarok. Under Hindu mythology he was considered to be a minion of Shiva, the destroyer. The Aztecs called him the sixth sun. The advent of the printing press brought the legend notoriety, notably in the practices of secret sects and societies.

Scholars who chronicle these secret circles report that the Golden Man is the return of the Christ, and the arrival of the Christian apocalypse. These claims remain controversial, at best. Other factions consider the Golden Man to be the Antichrist himself.

What is known about the Golden Man through my own research over the past five decades is that he will arrive bathed in beauty, and his proportions and symmetry are capable of stealing the breath away from the common man. The Golden Man is a prisoner to his own skin, but he shall also free himself from it. The nature of the Golden Man and his origin will remain one of mankind's best-kept secrets. But if he is permitted to fulfill his human and metaphysical potential, he will bring about the end of the world as we know it.

In all my years researching this phenomenon of culture and folklore, the answer to the following question has always eluded me: Is the Golden Man a creature that is created or self-made?

I turned the dusty paperback in my hands and reclined further back on my bed.

The stories inside the book wound inside each other, and many of them contained a story within a story like nested Russian dolls. I found myself returning to many of its passages and pages filled with poetry, incomprehensible diagrams and long passages filled with riddles and mathematical theorems.

I googled the author Salvatore Argento, but all I got was a short wiki page showing he had been alive during the late 19th century, working as a translator of medieval manuscripts and classic works, moving from city to city like a migratory bird. He had lived in Buenos Aires, Morocco, New York, Providence, and New Orleans. According to the page, he had gone mad around 1898 of unknown causes, and he had died in a sanitarium in San Francisco. He was said to have exchanged angry letters with Lovecraft, one of his publishing rivals at the time.

Winter pelted the streets outside with snow this morning, and I opted for a quiet Saturday in bed. The radiators cast bright heat throughout the apartment. I lay on the mattress just in my briefs. My meaty, muscled thighs were pinched at the hip by the tight underwear, and a patch of dark hair trailed up to my hairy chest. I supposed I needed to buy underwear a couple of sizes bigger now, but I had no idea when I was going to stop growing. I sighed.

I needed this down time, I needed time to think about my options.

A month ago, I had spent a long weekend in Nathan's condo in Los Angeles, a place I had started to think of as the White Pyramid, because every architectural detail of the place rose into the peak of the hill like an Egyptian tomb. It was there that he had ball-gagged me, tied me down, locked down my cock, whipped me, and taught me what it meant to serve a master. I had crossed over into a new territory of my sexual pleasures, and he had made many of my fantasies come true. Yet something was missing. Something about my visit felt wrong, but it took me time to think about what it was that didn't sit right with me.

When he had denied me the ability to cum, I had complied, but the days in Kansas City after my return were torture. I had jerked off in my apartment, in the toilet at work, at the gym, but I could not make myself feel the pleasure of a deep orgasm anymore. Nathan had a hold on me I could not explain, and in my newly transformed body, I felt incomplete without the ability to spill my seed into my hand.

These were the rules he had made for me.

I grabbed my pile of comics from the nightstand. On each one of these, men graced the covers in the middle of the action as they flew and burst through brick walls. Their muscles were piled thick and tight over their frames, and the skintight costumes they wore made my cock stir, the way it had when I was 12 years old, playing with myself in my bedroom at my parents' house.

There was something about the costume itself that drew me to these pages. Take The Overfiend, from Liberty Comics, for example. The Overfiend had started out as a line cook from Houston, Texas, and a radioactive blast inside a submarine during the Cold War turned him into a superhuman with god-like strength, heat vision, and a healing factor that rendered him unkillable.

The Overfiend wore one of the most classic examples of these suits. His white boots came up to his knee, and the bulging calf muscles swelled with power. Each thigh filled out his black shiny tights to the very end of the elastic material, and the artist had drawn each quadriceps and hamstring with elegance and masculinity. Then came the white brief, perfectly contoured to his sprinter's ass, firm, round, hard as oak. The brief came down in a V shape through the front, defaulting in a thick bulge that promised a nice set of cock and balls. The artists didn't often draw the penis head or the separation of the balls, but my imagination filled in those details plenty of times, and The Overfiend's white trunks had caused many spills of cum during my reading time over the years. I always imagined myself putting my tongue right up to that smooth surface, ready to see what lay beneath the stretchy fabric.

Then came the rest of the black leotard. The pen of the artist had created the most perfect lines that rose up and out from The Overfiend's waist (which was punctuated with a black belt). His back muscles popped throughout he black spandex and spread out into a wide back — a wide set of lats that rose up into the air and supported his bulging arms and his rounded, firm shoulders. The neck was particularly hot. The way the fabric caressed the thick yoke of his trapezius and cinched his bull neck tight made me want to yank my meat until I came. But I had to be patient. There was more to see yet. The Overfiend's torso was held in tightly by a shredded set of abs that the black spandex could barely contain. The flat surface of his torso ended at his chest, a massive monument of muscle and tendon. The fabric was drawn by the artists with care, as if it were spun of the finest silk. The suit hid the nipples, but I imagined silver-dollar-sized orbs that I could have licked for hours on end. And the suit ended at the neck, cinched tight, allowing The Overfiend to see and breathe but containing his Adonis proportions inside a tight layer of black fabric. Branded into his forehead was a symbol that resembled a nine-pointed star, inked in black and green.

I turned the pages on issue number 537, featuring one of the classic covers of The Overfiend. He lay spread-eagled, on a mountain top, injured, while an army jet fired down upon him from the clouds. This morning, I was laid out on my bed in a similar pose, my bulge pointing upward, just like The Overfiend.

Lately, I was sleeping longer and longer, and on the nights when I experienced my growth spurts, I could often sleep as much as twelve hours. This time, I had already slept for ten, but the gray snowstorm that was raking over the Missouri sky made me drowsy. I could never remember my dreams, but this time, as I dove into a black pillow of sleep, I had a dream that for the first time, came as clearly to me as waking life.

Here is what I dreamt.

I came to my senses, slowly, like a fluorescent buzzing to full power. I could see a flat mesa that resembled those in the state of Arizona, a state I have never visited in my life. The sky was so pale it looked white, and I was naked. I lay flat on my back, but the sun was blinding me, and I stood up. As I did so, I realized this mesa was elevated several hundred feet off the canyon floor. The sun whitewashed my skin, pale skin covered in the downy blond hairs I had always known.

A horn rang in the sky, like a beast's war cry, and the sky grew paler, almost white. The horns made music that filled me with dread, and the clouds on the horizon resembled a beast, a dragon, a creature with lips snarled and teeth curled to devour.

My body changed.

My muscles inflated and enlarged, and as they did so, my skin ripped open. There was never any blood. This was the ripping of my waking reality. Below me, I could see my cock and balls change, too. My previous dick, seven inches and narrow, gorged itself with new tissue, and it thickened up, and its mushroom head darkened. My mound of blond pubic hair went black. Runes and hieroglyphics appeared on the shaft, like tattoos inked with tar. Then they vanished. My body swelled.

The changes to my musculature were familiar by now. In real life I had been changing this way for weeks, but in the dream, this metamorphosis was sped up to a span of minutes.

My bull tits were nothing but hard muscle. My ripped stomach was strong, taut, my legs and ass powerful like Hercules. The hair that grew on my chest, legs, and arms was coarse and dense, like I had always dreamed of as a kid. The horn in the sky blasted again, and a pulse of green light bore down on the mesa. I shielded my eyes as a wave of energy blew me back.

When I moved my arm, The Overfiend stood in front of me. His costume made my loins burn with pleasure. My cock went hard just looking at his suit, the way the tight black unitard tucked right into his tall boots, the way the briefs hugged his bulge hanging down from his white briefs, the way his forearms rippled with muscle and his white gloved hands clenched, making his pecs tighten up against his muscled body. His heat vision could burn through rock and metal, and his eyes glowed perpetually green.

In the dream, he knew me. And he called me by my name.

"Roland, the invincible Roland," he said. "What brings you to these canyons?"

The Overfiend had always played a bit of a mercenary in the comics, and this time it was no different. I couldn't trust him.

He stepped closer, and my sexual hunger came alive as I saw each muscle, each shift of his cock and balls as he closed the distance between us.

"I am not really sure myself," I said. I didn't know why I was here, but I wasn't going to lie. I still believed in the truth. "Maybe you can help me figure it out."

I walked toward him. The cleft in his chin, his light stubble, the scar over his left eye, they were just like I had always remembered from the pages of the comic.

"Well, only heroes come to this place. It's a canyon for initiations. This is the Canyon at the End of the World. Others have stood where you stand today. Most notably The Fighter, the world's best-known mutated human."

The Fighter had been my childhood hero. He was in a sense even more arousing than The Overfiend, and I looked around the flat rocks for a sign of his cape and his handsome face. A wind stirred, and a dust cloud blew toward the horizon. As far as I could tell, I was alone here with The Overfiend. The Fighter was the most noble of all the heroes, a man who lived by the truth. A man whose veins ran with lava, and whose compassion knew no limit. He was a real hero.

The Overfiend was neither villain nor hero. He lived in a world of shifting morality and endless adaptation. He laughed often at himself and at the men who fell for his deceptions. In Liberty comics, The Overfiend had the best bits of knowledge, but always at a price.

I needed answers from The Overfiend.

"So, this place revealed something to The Fighter. Tell me what it reveals for me," I said.

"I'm afraid it's not much, Roland," The Overfiend said, "just little bits, and bits, and bits. Microscopic bits. Itty bits." His voice danced with mockery, and he smiled like the Cheshire Cat. Fuck, he was handsome. "But what is true is that you have triggered an ability inside of you, initiating you into the legions of men like me or The Fighter."

The Overfiend walked toward me. I could see his cock and balls shift from side to side as his briefs tried to contain his bulge.

"But what am I?" I said. He was now just inches from my face. I could for the first time see the ridge between his hard pecs, and the erect points of his nipples. His lips looked soft, and his stubble rough as sandpaper. I wanted that stubble on my balls.

"I will tell you what you are not," The Overfiend said. He put both arms on my shoulders, and my cock came dangerously close to his midsection. I was taller than him by several inches, thanks to my transformation. I wanted to touch his spandexed body so badly. But I waited till he finished.

"You, my friend, are not like most of us. Not part of the inner circle quite yet, are you? Yeah, you're a long way away from the merchandise, the sponsorships, the publicists. *The free clothes."* He laughed, but this time he cackled only with his eyes.

"You have not been bitten by radioactive scorpions," he said. "You did not fall out of a spaceship from a mission to the outer galaxy, and you did not alter your DNA to become a superhuman. You are not a mutant, whether self-made or triggered by science. You, my friend, are not a conventional superhero."

"Everything changed from the time I was stabbed," I said. The Overfiend considered this information, and he moved in close to my face. His eyes deepened in color.

He kissed me, exploring my mouth with his full lips. My thick cock brushed up against the silky but strong material of his suit, and I could feel my muscles tense up. After he kissed me, he took my face in his hands.

"So… here's your news bulletin. Feel free to tweet as you wish, just be sure to give me the credit," The Overfiend said. "You are the harbinger of the end of the world, friend. It all starts with you. Your body is perfect, an amalgam of the perfect proportions. The most symmetrical and powerful human being to walk the earth in a long time. But the end of times — it all starts with you," he said.

He laughed, and there were tears in his eyes. These were not tears of sympathy. They were tears of pity, and of mockery, too. I felt his pity for me, and I could also tell he wanted to fuck. He wanted me.

"But what do I do? How can I stop the end of the world?" I said.

"That's up to you get to figure out, brother," he said. "Better renew that library card. Hurry hurry, no time to worry." He shifted his weight from one foot to another. He was dancing. "There have been others like you before, who have mastered the systems of the universe, and they have also had the chance to bring the end of the world about. But they didn't do so. As of today, it has yet to happen. But if it's going to happen, it's gonna be only you. You will be the person that triggers the apocalypse. So, in a way, you're at this all by your little old self."

The Overfiend had always been smug, but I no longer thought he was funny. Not at all. In fact, I felt like he needed a bit of discipline to put him in his place. I felt fear and frustration, and his words stung. I didn't want to think these things were true. I tried to remind myself I was only in a dream, but this felt real, and the rage I felt was real, too. My body was sweating under the white sun, and sweat dampened the dark hair on my forearms and legs.

I wanted him to stop laughing. To stop mocking me. I took over The Overfiend.

I grabbed the rogue superhero's hands from my shoulders, where he had been resting them, and I squeezed his fists inside mine, not hard enough to break bone, but to make him feel pain. He winced and fell down to his knees immediately. The view of his chiseled body fueled my cock with urgency, and I pulled him toward me and forced my thick dick into his mouth. I towered over him.

My prick was much too large for him to take in, but I yanked hard on his arms and pulled him down on it. The shaft made it down his throat, and he moaned with the pleasure of danger. The sun shone right on his black suit, and it gave off a metallic sheen as the muscles in his neck flexed in order for him to swallow my cock.

The Overfiend's eyes made contact with mine, and though he was gagging on my dick, his eyes pleaded for more. I let go of his arms and gave them a break. I grabbed his shoulder-length brown hair and jammed his face into my crotch. His chest shook with excitement, and he worked his way up and down my dick.

I pulled The Overfiend back up, and I turned him around so he could look up at the flat Arizona mesas while I put him in a headlock. His dick was alive and hard, straining against the layers of high-tech fabric, a stiff rod straining against his white trunks. "Let me go," he pleaded, and my shaft slid right between his legs. He started riding it, breathing hard and soaking his uniform with his sweat. He clamped down on my cock with his thighs and begged for it. The headlock was tight, and his two puny arms around the vice made of my forearms was futile. I pressed my naked dick against the spheres of his ass, and I ground my hips forward. The white fabric kissed the head of my dick, and I went deep between his ass cheeks. If I pressed any further, I would rip through his tights and into his hole.

I took the opportunity and pushed my hips forward. The head of my dick pressed against his skintight uniform and in between his cheeks, but the material did not break. Not yet. My dick went in deep. He screamed with burning pain and wet pleasure.

The Overfiend strained against my headlock, and the veins in his neck bloomed forth. His heat vision went off, and rays of energy shot from his eyes into the wide-open canvas of the canyon. I didn't want him to pass out, but I did want to show him my power. I released him from the headlock as I tossed him onto the surface of the mesa. Even in the dream I couldn't control my own superhuman strength, and The Overfiend skidded on the rocks, which scraped skin off his right cheek and scuffed the smooth shine off his costume. He sprang back up to his feet immediately, his erection still pointing toward me. He panted. A rivulet of blood coursed down his temple.

"Then the prophecies are true," said The Overfiend, as he walked back toward me. "Some new master of the Process has been sent here."

I had heard the Process mentioned before, by Victor, in the real world, when I had landed in Los Angeles. But in the dream, I couldn't remember exactly what it was or how it worked.

"Tell me what you know about the Process," I said.

"The master of the Process always has the key to the end of the world in his hands. That's to say, there has to be a teacher for every Golden Man, and the teacher is the keeper of the Process. The Golden Man learns it from him. It's as simple as that. The old master is just that, old. Old, like those old legends. Fuck the old ones, I say. That's what makes the Golden Man. But the new flesh, like you, I can believe in that. Now show me what they teach you and show me how you like to harness a man's flesh, boy."

No one except Nathan called me boy. I felt a certain rage toward this former childhood icon and his cynicism. I was sick of his mockery. *You're in a dream,* I reminded myself, *so act like it and figure it out, Roland.*

And so I did. In all the years I had plunged deep into my fantasies, the hero's costume, the skinsuit, the jumpsuit, the catsuit, had burned itself into my memory, and my fetish for these suits had intensified the older I became. Now, as I stalked this superhero in his own skinsuit of shiny material, I channeled my aggression into a mental image of his suit and that of every superhero's suit I had ever seen in my life.

I walked toward The Overfiend, and as I did so, I willed my own skinsuit to issue itself forth over me. The thought came from a black space in my mind. It came from the very vacuum that produced the golden symbols and the cities of geometric shapes. It was a solid thought. A hard thought.

And under that white sky, I created my own skinsuit over my body.

This was no spandex uniform like The Overfiend's or The Fighter's. It was better. Fitted around every muscle, thin as a sheet of rubber, and strong like carbon fiber.

The suit spilled forth from the slits on my skin, and it covered me in a matter of seconds, covering my toes, feet, legs, ass, chest, and back. Its color was the bluest shade of gray I had ever seen. It shone under the sun like a polished stone. It encased each of my fingers better than a custom glove. My cock was sheathed in the suit, and my thick member bulged forth from it. My march forward was calculated, precise, and in perfect sync with the pace of time.

The Overfiend was only about twenty feet away now. Delight drew a smile on his face from ear to ear.

"Only the masters can spin a suit like yours. You are the real deal.," he said.

The Overfiend offered himself at my feet and he put his lips to my bulge, pressing his mouth and nose up to the thin material, through which I could feel every sensation as if it were my own skin. He nuzzled my balls, and when he was done, he propped himself on a nearby rock, belly down and ass up in the air. It was his ultimate act of submission.

The Overfiend removed his belt, where I know he kept many of his weapons. The back of his body was strong, taut with sinew and muscle, like a gymnast's. I could see the hole in his white briefs where I had penetrated his sacred costume. I wanted this body.

Using my hands, I ripped the white briefs off his tight ass. Underneath, his black unitard offered him one last layer of protection, and I could see his ass quiver under the sun. I grabbed a patch of his uniform with my right hand and pulled upward, ripping it off the body in a microsecond, sending it in all directions like black confetti.

I knelt down, and I put my cock in the cleft of his cheeks. He moaned a word, and he clenched his fists as I put the tip of my bulge right on the rosebud of his ass. I still had my suit on. *How do I get this off me?* I thought. But the suit was one step ahead of me, because it peeled itself back from my cock and balls, leaving the rest of me bathed in its gray-blue membrane. The suit gave in to my thoughts, and I was certain that it was nothing more than an extension of my body. This I would have to investigate some other time, in some other dream.

I fucked The Overfiend in a smooth pattern of thrust and release, feeling his sweat come into contact with my skin. Slabs of muscle shifted in his back, and he thanked me for fucking him, he thanked me for being strong and powerful and masculine. He thanked me for taking control of him on that lonely mesa in the desert. I spanked him several times on his round ass cheeks, and my brute force brought up red welts to their creamy surface. As they got redder, he groaned with more pleasure.

I had never felt so in control, and I wanted this moment under the sun to show me more about this thing called the Process. I wanted to fuck The Overfiend all day and all night, for seven days and seven nights. His body was mine, and I felt close to cumming. I would never tire of controlling a submissive hero like The Overfiend, and my body had the endurance to do so. The Overfiend bucked his hips under my thrusts, and when I came inside him, he screamed at the top of his lungs. He came at the same time, too, his semen running down the rock. Scorpions emerged from the pores of the rock and crawled over the white liquid. I wiped the cum off the rock with my gloved hand and smeared it on his right cheek. He lay very still. From the other side, on his left cheek, a scorpion crawled toward his eye. "You're mine," I said.

The clouds turned a deep rose color, then red as blood, and then I awoke.

◆

The dream left me back in my bed in Kansas City. I looked at the clock. I had been asleep for twelve hours, and it was now 8 pm. I had only ever experienced pleasure when I was under Nathan's control, but this dream had been the reverse. And why The Overfiend?

I blinked, and a sharp pain wound itself between my pecs. The hair and skin looked normal, but there was a wrongness there, something red-hot. A burning.

My heart was beating, and I felt electric shocks in my chest. If I didn't know any better, I thought I might be going into cardiac arrest. Something was wrong, and I might have no other choice than to go to the hospital. I wasn't afraid to go into an ER, but I had certainly avoided it for months.

I got out of bed and walked toward the bathroom. The light was dim, and my head grew heavy. Maybe I had slept too long? I felt seasick and sleep-sick at the same time.

I walked into the bathroom that night to inspect myself, and when I saw my reflection in the mirror, I took a good look for a second or two. Then I screamed like an animal, and I punched the bathroom mirror with my closed fist. My hand went through the wall, and it came out intact. I screamed again.

Behind me, I could see something move, and I saw my reflection in the full-length mirror I kept behind the door. I saw the monstrosity, the change in me, and I grabbed that mirror too, breaking it over my leg. Glass went everywhere, but it didn't make a single cut. I stumbled over to the hallway, and I reminded myself to keep quiet.

These were the days I was finalizing my flesh, the days in which I was truly becoming a monster. But I needed to remain calm, I told myself.

Last thing you want is to draw attention to yourself, Roland. No, the neighbors don't need to know anything about you other than the way your apartment stays quiet night and day. You need to hush.

Hush, Roland.

I slumped back against the wall, and I heard it groan as my muscular body sent cracks upward like spider webs. Bits of drywall fell onto my head and my face.

I cupped my face in my hands and tried to cry, but I couldn't. The days were long now, and I wished I had a family to confide in, parents to seek for wisdom. But there was just me.

Time passed there on the floor, and my breathing returned to normal eventually. Maybe I sat there for two hours, or maybe two days. But one thing was for sure: when I pulled my hands away, the changes I had seen in the bathroom were still there. There was no going back to my former self. I was in deep trouble.

I looked down at my bent knees, those hard knees like two granite boulders, and the thick thighs packed with agility and strength like a horse. I looked down at my calves, my feet. Starting from my toes, a blue-gray membrane covered my skin, pressed against me like the sleekest and sexiest liquid metal I had ever seen. It adhered to my feet, calves, and ass, and it even covered my bulge, just like one of the latex catsuits Nathan liked to encase me in. The second skin stopped at about halfway up my stomach, and that was farther along than when it had stopped at my waist, when I broke the mirrors in the bathroom. It had spread. The suit caught the hallway light and gave it a sheen like it was bathed in hard sunlight.

I was covered in half a skinsuit, and as hard as I tried pulling on it, it wasn't coming off. I screamed again.

There was only one person to call. I walked to the end table in my living room and dialed him up.

"Roland," Nathan said. "I know why you're calling."

"Something's happening to my body," I said.

"Then it's important that you don't tell anyone. Don't tell the cops, don't tell the hospital, holy fuck, don't even think of hospitals right now. You will likely be tracked. You need to go invisible."

"But these changes—"

"—Save it, save it for when we're not on a phone line that can be traced. I'll call you on another line to tell you when we can meet next. Just sit back and work with me. Be patient."

I hung up. This time I did cry when I collapsed on the floor.

CHAPTER 9
THE GOLDEN MAN AND THE MONASTERY

Kirby stopped by my cubicle early in the morning, before the other staff arrived on the floor. He threw his weight right on top of the desk, and his thigh spilled over, like lava seeping down a mountaintop. As the head of the hospital, he gave himself permission to intrude on everyone's space, metaphorically but also physically.

"Slim," he said, "let me ask you something. You been juicing?"

My skin crawled and I stared into his flat eyes.

"Excuse me?"

"People have been talking," he said, waiting for me to say something in protest. But I kept my lips shut. "I don't care what you do on your own time, but I have to ask, for your sake. Are you on something?"

"Like what?" I said.

"Human growth hormone, T?"

"Of course not."

"Look at you, though. You're popping out your shirt."

Kirby was right. My scrubs, which had once been loose as pajamas, were now skintight. I had tried finding new sizes that would fit me, but for now, I was still wearing them snug. The trousers bunched at my crotch, and my biceps threatened to pop out of my sleeves at all times. I had been too busy to go buy a new, larger set.

"It's always been my job to be the honest one around here," Kirby said. "You're freaking everyone out. The women. The men."

"What do you mean?" I said. All these weeks, I had endured the glances of puzzlement from the rest of the staff. Had they been discussing my appearance all this time?

"These clothes, they're inappropriate. And we don't have rules here about how men should wear their hair, but your dye job calls too much attention," Kirby said. He leaned in closer. "We're not running a rent-boy business, okay? If you ever try to repeat this to another person, I'll deny I was ever even here at your desk, but I will tell you this now: It's time to stop this whore shit, faggot."

Some things you are never prepared for. I blinked in shock.

"I want you to go get a proper-fitting pair of pants," Kirby said. "Sue told me you split them at a staff meeting."

"I did."

It was true. Just a couple of days before, Sue Marnie, the other head RN besides myself, had dropped her tablet as we walked into a meeting, and I had stopped to pick it up. My trousers had split from my crack all the way up to the small of my back as the muscle of my buttocks pushed through. The black Speedo I wore underneath had kept me from her seeing me naked, but that had made it worse. The day I dreamed about The Overfiend, I woke up from the dream partially covered in a skinsuit made of a tough metallic membrane. If it hadn't been for Nathan, I might have panicked and checked myself into the hospital. But his voice had remained calm and in control. He had talked me through the next steps, and I was grateful to him. Over a secure phone line, Nathan had advised me to take a few painkillers and sleep it off. He had me take deep breaths on the phone , and I lay down in my bed, as the skinsuit glinted under the moonlight coming in through my window blinds. I finally dozed as he talked to me over the line. The next morning, the suit was gone. I was relieved, but I also missed the sexual pleasure of seeing a tight sheath of metal cover my musculature. The skinsuit had been real, and the fear it triggered in me was real, but there was another feeling inside me that I could not identify. That feeling was addictive, and full of pleasure. As I got ready for work, I rummaged in my drawers. The speedo I used for swimming reminded me of the skinsuit to some extent, and I slid it over my beastly thighs to use as underwear. Its compression and its blue sheen were good enough to help me remember the terror, and the uncanny pleasure I had felt that night. The swimsuit wasn't proper underwear, and it was a dead giveaway that I was a perv, at least in Sue's mind. Oh, Sue had laughed and laughed, and so had the other two interns in the room. But Sue was known for reporting exactly this kind of thing, even while pretending to be nonchalant. I am not sure what her report had said, but now I knew it had rolled all the way up to Kirby. She had gone straight to the top with her complaint.

"We can't have indecent exposures like that here," he said. "You might think it's funny, but we're here to work and not play sick games. If there's anything illegal, or if you're swiping gear from the pharmacy, your fucking days are numbered."

Kirby's upper lip was dotted with sweat. I felt him scanning the thatch of chest hair poking from my shirt. He looked like he wanted to punch me, or fuck me, or both. I found him repulsive.

"Won't happen again," I said, using the toughest voice I could muster. I was angry.

I went back to my monitor, hoping Kirby would get the message. He did. After a few seconds, he left.

That afternoon, things took a turn for the worse.

As a general rule, I don't work in the ER. I did, many years ago, but I found the intensive care unit to suit me better.

It was a Thursday, and it was always on that day of the week that we were short on staff. The ER needed backup. A Mack truck spun on black ice on the highway and rammed into a car. Fifteen cars piled up as a result, and 14 victims came into Arkum that night. The ER had plenty of patients to keep the whole team busy, and I gave it my best.

As I finished switching out an IV, I heard a crash and the sound of crumpling metal and glass breaking. Many people shouted, and their bellows were coming from the driveway I had just left. Something really bad was happening out there.

"There's been an accident in the side entrance!" shouted someone. The side entrance was where ambulances and EMTs came into Arkum. An accident out there couldn't be a good thing, especially if more victims from the pileup were still being brought in.

I knew what to do. I ran to the driveway to see what was happening.

I burst through the double doors onto the driveway, and I saw metal cubes, broken glass, and liquid everywhere. A flatbed had been delivering large metal containers full of medical supplies. Each of these boxes had to weigh at least 80 pounds. I estimated there had been probably about 50 boxes stacked on the back of the truck, and they had spilled out of its side. Some boxes had split open, and glass and liquid had exploded from their open lids.

Men shouted, and I saw two of the paramedics pushing on a pile of the steel boxes. They had fallen right on top of one of the delivery men who had been working with the boxes. He was crushed under the metal, and his eyes had rolled to the back of his head as he went into shock. The metal pinned his legs, all the way past his waist. The other delivery man was there next to his injured partner, and a few onlookers formed a half circle around the accident.

"Give us a hand," his partner shouted to me.

I moved quickly, ready to save the man's life. He was bleeding profusely, and it was likely that the broken bones in his body could have perforated vital organs. I lunged for the boxes and found a hold for my hands. I concentrated in order to generate the brute strength I needed from my body, but I didn't have to. My legs came to a standing position with ease, and my arms pulled the stack of steel containers into the air. Moving the objects felt as easy as re-stacking a column of pillows. I moved one, two, three, all the way up to seven boxes that had fallen on top of the man.

I felt my flesh swell with force, and my skin made a thin ripping sound. There was nowhere I could set the boxes down except the landscaped garden, and I set them down gently. I moved one box at a time, faster than any other man there could have done so. My arms handled the weight with precision. This was way too easy. Then I heard the other EMTs scream. They scooped up their teammate and prepared him to be rushed into our ER.

I stood up from squatting. I looked around the circular driveway. As the two paramedics took the injured man through the sliding doors, I was left outside, alone. I did what felt like instinct. I walked back into the ER, ready to help out some more.

As I walked, I saw the faces around me go white with shock, and several of the women recoiled, leaning back. The men stared at me, first in the face, then lower. And then lower. They were horrified. Someone shouted, "Roland, get the fuck over here!" And they beckoned me toward the administrative office. I still didn't know what was wrong, until I looked down.

I was naked, from neck to my ankles. Beneath me, tattered ribbons from my scrubs hung to my waist. My jockstrap had also ripped off, and I was naked. Hairy, swollen with muscle, and naked. Only my feet remained covered, in their socks and their crepe-soled shoes. I had literally exploded from my scrubs. Now my nakedness was all these onlookers could see. I spotted a couple of nurses from my team, and a surgeon who knew me well. Their astonishment was palpable as my hairy, muscled body throbbed with adrenaline. As dozens of eyes inspected my body, I felt clumsy and ugly. I walked toward the administrative offices, then ran back to the locker rooms, where I had my change of clothes. I left work immediately, too dumbfounded and too embarrassed to come back.

◆

Winter can be harsh in Kansas City, and in this part of the country, the days are short, while nights are long.

After my incident at Arkum Memorial, I knew I had to find another place to work. My days back at work were uncomfortable. I endured many jokes. Snickers in the hallways became a common practice each time I walked by. I took the stairs, as always, hoping to be left alone.

Most of my co-workers gave me a wide berth now, and many avoided direct eye contact. The ones that didn't liked to stare at me for a long time. I felt their eyes on my dark hair, on my shoulders and arms. I felt their gaze rove over my face, looking for signs of an explanation in my eyes.

The job I had applied for requested recommendations from my

superiors, and when Kirby caught wind of it, he got on the phone with the administrator of the other hospital. I don't know what he said to them, but a day later, I was sitting at my desk when I got a phone call from them saying they were turning me down for the position.

If I applied for another nursing job in a twenty-mile radius, all my references would lead right back to Arkum Hospital, back to my old life. And Kirby would tell them stories that weren't true. He would tell them I wasn't fit to work somewhere else.

That afternoon I put in my request for a leave of absence. Kirby approved it immediately.

The new hospital had passed me up, and my current team was passing me up, too. The world was moving on.

I began my leave of absence, and I spent most of it indoors, thinking, looking over the logs of vital stats I had recorded while I witnessed my transformation. I never stopped recording this data, because I was hopeful that medicine could help me someday if I kept detailed records. I no longer had access to blood tests, but at least I could monitor everything else on my own. I felt solitude, and it was as solid as a real object. I thought a lot about my past.

Solitude was never something I really wanted, but here I was, surrounded by it. I was grateful for my two ex-boyfriends. Those were good times in their company, even if one of them cheated on me and the other one simply fell out of love with me. There was Nathan, too, but I was not sure what to call him. Certainly not a boyfriend.

I had two real loves in my life.

First there had been Grey, and after him, Smith. With each one, they sucked my cock, and I sucked theirs. I let both of them fuck me, but the pains inside my ass always led us to awkward conversations, and we turned away from each other in bed. Shame and frustration. It was a cycle we knew well. I loved those two men, but I never had the courage to tell either one of them that there was a part of me that wanted to get tied up, to get spanked with a paddle, to be bound in unthinkable positions, and to be humiliated like a servant while getting fucked.

I never asked those two men for the domination I craved.

I never once told them that even though we only had vanilla sex, I might want to fuck them in the ass one day, too. For years, I gave up mine, but what I wanted was a piece of leather stretched between us, or a mesh of latex, the skintight bodysuit of a superhero to bridge our sexual play. But even today, years after our breakup, they knew nothing about what made me tick.

I wasn't good at keeping in touch with people, but I knew both Grey and Smith had other boyfriends now. They had other lives. I considered picking up the phone to talk to them, but I didn't actually know what I would like to say to either one. I never called.

I craved discipline, I craved the forces of superhero and villain rocking back and forth in a tug-of-war. I craved aggression in the form of a muscled man who owned me with his eyes.

◆

I spent four weeks alone this way. One of the nice perks of being a workaholic that never takes time off is that when you finally decide to take a leave of absence, your employer has no choice but to say yes. Kirby had signed off on the leave of absence with pay. I was glad. But it wasn't an endless leave. In two more weeks, my leave would end, and one thing was for sure. I would not be coming back.

I had savings in my bank account, and I knew how to live lean. I only needed fresh air, food, and access to sex. These things I could find easily and within my means, and I could live on my own, this way, for a good year.

I found out how to meet men on Craigslist. Quick encounters in their bedrooms, or sometimes in a rented hotel room. I also learned how to target a good partner in a bar, how to move in close to him, how to smile, and how to use my fortress of a body to give them what they wanted, so I could get what I wanted.

I never exchanged phone numbers with these men, and I never pushed their limits very far. I kept the hoods and the ball gags deep in my trunk at my bed.

I never brought men home. I needed to protect the solace I felt in my two-bedroom apartment. But I went out to meet these men. I just wanted their sex, plain and simple.

For now.

So, I had a way to live, to be outdoors, and to satiate the urges of my cock.

The one thing I couldn't live without was my calling. I was going to hold on to my profession as hard as I could. I just needed time to figure out how. Life wasn't any good to me without providing medical care for those who needed it. The thought of no longer helping people made me ill to my stomach. In my time as a professional, I helped women overcome breast cancer treatments. I held a baby's torn finger in place as a surgeon sewed it back onto his hand. I worked on soldiers who came back without hands from Iraq after improvised explosive devices tore them to shreds. I aided people to find a little more time on earth as they prepared to die, and I had helped others, the ones who were too deep inside diseased states, die in peace.

I loved my job, but the only way to get back to what I love was to disappear, and to gather my thoughts. Kansas City had too much noise, too much familiarity. It has too many memories of Roland, blond Roland, reedy

Roland, the former me.

Perhaps if I traveled far away, I could show up in another city and start all over again. Charlotte. Portland. Austin. There were about two dozen states where I didn't need to get a new nursing license, but even if I had to take the examinations, it was worth it. I wasn't sure how I would get around the personal references dilemma. But I was willing to do whatever it took to do so.

If I stayed in Kansas City, I would always have to deal with the stares from people, and the disapproval of my peers. I would be a freak, through and through.

The guy who turned into a juicer. The guy who put on a nude show while on the job. The perv.

I have to disappear, I thought.

On a brisk winter morning, I walked into the hospital and took the elevator to the third floor. It was much too early for too many people to notice. I made small talk with some of the doctors and nurses who were doing rounds, and they were polite, friendly. I felt ill at ease in my triple-extra-large parka and my baggy size 38 jeans. I walked over to my cube and gathered my things. My legs swam under the blue denim, but they kept people from staring at my massive thighs, my gargantuan bubble ass.

A few books, my address book, a few notepads, and some reference materials. I jotted down my computer passwords, and I left my single plant at the receptionist's desk.

I walked out of the hospital into the early stages of a blizzard, which had been scheduled to arrive later this afternoon, according to radio reports.

That was the last time I ever set foot in Arkum Hospital.

That night at home, I emptied out my drawers and trashed all my old clothes. I mailed off eight more checks to cover the rest of my rent through the end of my lease, and I packed a single backpack with two sets of jeans and shirts, my razor, and my passport. The hospital owed me accumulated back pay, and with direct deposit, I would be able to tap into that cash from any place outside Kansas City.

I was ready to disappear.

I went to the back porch of my apartment, and I poured myself a tall whiskey. Nowadays, alcohol had the effect of tap water on my body, but I liked the taste. The book *The Golden Man,* by Salvatore Argento, lay on my lap. I had placed colored paper flags in my favorite chapters, and I put my finger in the cleft of the book's pages and flipped it open to read.

Excerpt from *The Golden Man: A Gay Bondage Manual,* by Salvatore Argento, 1898.

The lore surrounding the tales of the Golden Man in the centuries past presents some of the most puzzling and paradoxical portraits of its myth. A historian's work is never done until every stone is turned, and no investigation into the Golden Man should be complete without visiting the Catholic Church and its legacy. It is in the works of the Vatican and the institution of the Papist church that we find one of the most lurid legends of the Golden Man and the strange allure he held over men who may have been privy to his existence.

These tales, dear reader, come to me from wonderful research trips that have proven fruitful despite the dangers inherent in world travel. In these visits to old friends from an earlier phase of my academic past, I have come away with new findings. My friends, these scholars, whose names must remain invisible to every historian, have given me glances and peeks at the most pivotal works surrounding the Golden Man.

One of these legends tells the story of an illustrator who was living in Ireland at the time the Book of Kells was being produced. It is said this monk stole a handful of sheets of vellum.

These contraband blank pages found their way into Cordoba, Spain, where a certain friar lived amongst a colony of other men of the cloak. This friar had a tale to tell, and he bought the vellum, with the meager life savings he had accumulated as a man of the robe.

The friar wrote down a tale in these pages of vellum that chilled me the first time I read them in my friend's flat in London in spring. My friend, M_____, spread out the vellum sheets for me in his drawing-room, and left me to my own devices for days. It is there that I pieced together the story. With each piece of the puzzle, a sense of dread came over me, and I felt a chill course down my back, despite the copious amounts of tea my friend had sent to the drawing-room. But the tale held a spell over me, and I could not leave the chamber until I learned its secrets.

The tale itself left me with one eye open for many nights, sleepless, fearful of the dominion of dreamtime. I feared the nightmares that would come from this tale, and I feared something else. Some unknown presence understood I had read this clandestine tale, and this force lay outside my window, outside the safety of my rooms. Even years after that visit to London, I still fear for my safety. I feel a perpetual gaze in the ether, watching me.

I eventually returned to my home in San Francisco, and the distance warmed me with a certain comfort. San Francisco put me a world away from this lurid tale, and yet, I felt I should not have read the tale. I should have let things be as they were.

The best way to exorcise this feeling, this sense of being watched, is to put down the story, as best as I can relate it. Perhaps it will put some distance between me and its horrors.

I can see San Francisco bay from this window tonight, but even as I write these words down on paper, preparing them to be sent off to my publisher, I fear. I fear those who know about this tale, and I fear those who seek to suppress it. They may suppress my person, if I am not careful.

But a tale should not wait to be told, because sometimes it is like a ripe apple tethered to a tree. A tale, like an apple, means to find its ground, and that moment is now before me. Though there may not be direct access to the vellum manuscript today, I have synopsized the story here, in order to comply with the pressures that time places onto the cosmos and, in turn, the cosmos places on us. And so this story travels downward, guided by gravity, to connect with its ground.

The Tale of the Golden Man and the Monastery
In the year 1576, the Monastery of San Jerónimo housed 99 men of the robe. Inside its many towers, they manufactured inks for manuscripts and built furniture in all varieties of wood for the Church. Many of the pieces made in this monastery were said to be the best in Spain at the time. These pieces included steering wheels for ships, pulpits, and coffins for the royal crown of Spain.

Other objects were made in this monastery, too.

The men in this monastery built torture devices for the Inquisition, including manacles and the sharp nails used in the Iron Maiden. The monastery also produced copious honey to trade for other goods, and the wine they produced retained its sweetness, even when mixed with water.

During winter, a moribund dressed in rags knocked at the monastery door. The youngest friar opened the doors, as was the custom. The monastery provided sanctuary for all. The friar clutched his robes at the sight of the pilgrim at the door. The man's ragged hair trailed down his back like weeds and dry brush, and dried blood covered his exposed skin. He wore nothing more than a loincloth, and despite the harsh conditions of the wintery night, his skin was still warm. The friar brought him into the zaguán or patio. His dark skin glowed with a golden hue, and despite his sorry state, his face seduced every man there. It was a face made in the desert, with a heavy beard and eyes green like a lizard.

He's a Moor, shouted one of the friars.

I used to be a Moor, the man said. But I belong to no one anymore.

Surely you belong to the Lord, assured him the friars. A pair of friars washed the crusted skin off his arms and shoulders, revealing musculature unlike any they had ever seen before. Samson, whispered a few of the monks, cupping their hands to keep their words from ringing through the monastery. The monks who worked as transcript translators whispered other words. Hercules, they said, and genuflected.

The friars dressed the man's skin and found wounds on his flesh in various geometric shapes. Upon closer inspection, the shapes seemed to form a pattern. One friar dared touch the scars, and when he put his index finger to the circular mark, the stranger's skin exploded in a burst of white and gold light. For a brief moment, the power and the heat of the sun flooded the stone room, and then it vanished. The friars gasped. Demon, they whispered.

The youngest friar feared the giant brute, but an excitement rose inside him, and his eyes grew wide and bright.

The men brought the man to the sleeping quarters and dabbed his wounds, which by now had closed up. They bathed him in water, and with his permission, they sheared his locks. The youngest friar, the boy, saved the locks and hid them away under his pallet where he slept. The vision of the Moor put a spell on the young man, and when his eyes met the green points of the stranger's, he cast them downward, remembering he was just a monk, just a servant of God. There was no room for the carnal desires of the flesh inside the stone walls.

A spare robe was draped over the man's shoulders, but it couldn't properly cover his massive size. The rough brown fabric stretched across his chest, and its hem grazed the top of his knees. No one had ever seen a man of this scale in this part of the country before.

The friars brought the moribund to the dining hall, where they shared their bounty with him. He bit into mounds of bread and tasted small fish that shone like silver. He drank wine from their cups, and he wiped the drops with the back of his hand.

During this time, the abbot of the monastery had been busy in his quarters, writing letters to Carlos Ornelas, the patron of the abbey. The abbot, a man known for his razor sharp profile and his demand for cleanliness and discipline, enjoyed a direct link to Tomás de Torquemada, the Grand Inquisitor, but Ornelas was an important proxy, because the patron of the abbey was the one who reported back to the Inquisitor on the financial solvency of each monastery.

The abbot descended the stairs into the dining hall. When he saw the friars gathered around the dark-skinned stranger, he pressed his lips together and clapped his hands. The friars were trained in these hand signals. They dissipated like a flock of doves, and they went back to their cleaning duties.

The only friar who stayed next to the stranger was the youngest, who dared not touch the man's skin or his geometric wounds. He did crave his presence, and so he remained close.

The abbot ordered the young friar to place manacles on the stranger, and to bring him down to the monastery's dungeon. The friar did as he was told, though he knew men did not often survive the dungeon. It was here that the heretics were examined, punished, and drawn up like livestock. Many died at the hands of the abbot.

Do you denounce God?, the abbot asked the dark skinned stranger.

I am no demon, said the giant.

By the power of the holy church of God, I condemn you. Only until you repent will you have the opportunity to end your life of sin.

The abbot was known to become erect during these verdicts, and this time it was no different. He took a seat in a wide chair with a tall back. His long nose and deep brow gave him the semblance of a predatory bird, like a hawk perched on a rock. The abbot enjoyed performing the work of God this way. While the stranger was held down, he rubbed his loins through his robes, stifling his own grunts of self-pleasure.

The abbot ordered the stranger through every torture implement in the dungeon. The stranger was tied up by his wrists, and it took eight friars to raise him up in strappado. The stranger moaned and writhed, but he was much too strong for the torture. Ordinary men sometimes suffered broken wrists in the strappado, but the stranger's flesh remained taut and firm. His bones were strong, and he emerged intact from his bindings.

Next, the abbot ordered that the stranger be placed in the boots. The friars positioned his legs between two planks of oak, and they bound them by the ankles with rope and wedges. The strongest of the friars hammered the wedges, driving them closer together. As they did so, the wood began to squeak under the pressure of the hammer. The stranger's legs were much too strong for the pressure, and on the tenth strike, the oak wedges cracked into splinters. The abbot felt a deep pleasure in seeing men put through these procedures, but the essence of pain was indispensable.

The moribund felt pain, but he was much too strong to wince and cry in a manner that would pleasure the abbot.

Send him to the wheel, ordered the abbot. The men tied the stranger to a wooden wheel, and he complied, not once resisting. He was bound by his hands and feet to the gigantic wooden wheel. They tied his feet to the ground, so that when the friars turned the crank on the wheel, the pressure of the wood on a man's back would break his bones and joints. Strip his clothes, ordered the abbot. The friars tore the robes off the stranger, and his member, large, and perfectly in balance with his perfect physique, came up to attention. The friars turned the wheel many times, but the man's limbs remained intact.

He is invincible, said the abbot. We cannot rest until this demon from hell is vanquished.

I am no demon, said the stranger.

The young friar watched this torture, and he felt tears roll down his face at the man's pain. He pulled his hood over his head to hide their salty traces.

The abbot stood from his chair that night and walked to the center of the dungeon. He placed his fingertips on the ebony table, and ordered the friars to remove all tools from it. Then, he had the stranger brought to the table, and with his hands bound behind his back and a thick rope placed onto his mouth like a bridle, the abbot took hold of the stranger at the hips and abused his flesh, many times over. When the man did not bleed, the monk cursed him, and he slapped his face over and over, though no marks emerged on his cheeks.

This demon's will cannot be broken in one night, the abbot said. And for that, we will bring him closer to God through the punishment he deserves.

The abbot ordered the men to chain the stranger in the cells beneath the dungeon, the cells reserved for murderers and other criminals. He was strong, but not strong enough to break the iron manacles.

Over the next few weeks, the abbot ordered more men to torture, bind, and gag the giant stranger, and the friars of uncertain character followed his instructions. Some inserted their members in his backside, while others used his mouth as a receptacle for their urges. Others bathed the man in their seed, while others, including the abbot, flogged him over and over with whips and paddles. They violated him hundreds of times.

The abbot continued sending letters to the patron of the abbey, patron Ornelas, but he never mentioned the supernatural beast he kept chained beneath the towers. When the archbishops visited the monastery in the Spring, the abbot and his friars remained silent about the prisoner they housed.

Each night, the young friar came down often to feed him bread and water. When he put the cup to the man's lips, the stranger would say thank you, and after he gulped down the liquid, they would kiss, the stones cold underneath their bodies. The young friar never dared remove the manacles, but he learned how to climb on top of the man and lay on top of him, holding on to his neck and shoulders. The stranger couldn't free his arms, but he nuzzled the young friar with his beard, and he loved him with his eyes.

Sometimes, the young friar would reach down with both hands to rub the man's member, gently and with love, until he would feel him shake like earth, and the stranger's breath would come in ragged spurts. Sometimes, he would glow and bathe the cell with a golden light, and the young friar was sure that he could feel something divine in the warm glow of the man's skin.

In the evenings, the abbot and his two dozen executioners would punish and ravage the giant against his wishes, calling him the names of beasts, and spilling wine, spit, and excrement over him while laughing until their bellies hurt.

But in the day, after the morning mass and chores were complete, the young friar tip-toed down the stairs into the cell.

The young friar and the giant kissed and touched this way for weeks. The young friar caressed the thick black hair on the stranger's chest, and without looking him in the eye, he asked, whence do you come from?

The stranger had nothing left to lose in life because he had already lost his freedom, and he took pity on the young man, who was the only person who showed him any kindness.

"I was a Moor once. I was born far from these lands, deep in the deserts. I studied the movement of the moon and the stars, and I inscribed my observations in paper that my father made. I spent twenty years investigating the passage of time, and my calculations showed me something marvelous: man could enter into another form, another plane, and he would do so as the future unfolded unto him. Using the magic found in the cosmos, man could come closer to the heavens, and in a sense, he could get closer to God.

"One night, as I rode my horse on a road much too deserted for a single man, I carried my notes to deliver to the mathematicians who lived in the cities of the west. They wanted to know what I had learned about the path of the stars, and the mysteries of the earth.

"While I crossed the desert, four men accosted me in the dark. Thieves. They had scimitars, and I had nothing. They cut me many times on my stomach, but especially on my back. During their attack, I said farewell to my father, for I knew these were my last moments on earth. The men left me bleeding in the cold of the desert, and they robbed me of my papers, my money, and even my clothes. I shut my eyes and wished as hard as I could on the magical calculations from my notes. The papers were gone, but the incantations remained in my memory. I chanted out loud into the air, and the blueness of the night faded to the color of emeralds for a few moments, and then a gold light blinded me.

"When I awoke the next day, I found my wounds had receded, and though weak, I could stand on my own two legs. Strength had come back into my body. I returned to my

city, and I made a vow to disappear from the eyes of other men. You see, I knew that if men hunted me, they might hunt my father, the paper-maker. He was my only family, and I set out to spare his life. And so I traveled on my own, avoiding cities as much as I could, living off the land and begging. As the years went by, I came to understand what had changed in me since the day I was robbed."

Did you die and return to the land of the living? asked the young friar.

"No, I remained alive; I know this now. But I set in motion the changes that bring the chaos of the cosmos closer to earth. And as I did so, my flesh grew, and my mind transformed. My ivory skin and brown eyes changed. I became darker, reaching the hue before you now, and my eyes became as green as the sky I saw in my solitary vision. I lost the freckles of my former fair skin. I became a giant, and I learned there were other powers locked inside of me. I walked into the desert, the mountains, and the woods, and I haven't stopped walking. I have traveled for many years on foot, alone. I walk in order to understand my loneliness. Until I arrived at his monastery, that is. The night you welcomed me here, I was attacked by a pack of wolves, and I welcomed their jaws. Perhaps they could put me out of my misery. But I know they could not. It takes more than a wolf to kill me."

The boy, that young friar, returned to his cell and cried into the straw of his pillow.

Later in the summer of that year, the abbot of the monastery grew irritated and bored by the stranger bound in the dungeon. Though he still abused of his flesh and violated him while bound and gagged, he feared the repercussions from the Church, and most of all, the Pope.

The abbot ordered the finest punishment of all. He ordered his men to mummify the stranger in linens and bury him alive in the graveyard behind the monastery. The man struggled, and the friars used extra lengths of calf leather to reinforce the white linens. He lay under the ground for a week.

To make sure he was dead, the abbot ordered the men to dig up the body and unwrap it. They removed the leather and linens from the head, and when they did so, they found the green eyed man alive, and on the verge of madness. To the abbot the moribund looked feral, and masculine, and also changed, like a beast. He hated the visage of the Arab, and he hated himself for housing a demon for so long.

And now, the final punishment comes said the abbot. This is the hand of God. This is your last chance to repent, heretic.

. I am no demon, said the stranger with the green eyes.

The abbot ordered his men to unwrap the stranger, and they brought six of their strongest axes. These were the axes they used to cut wood in the forest. That day, under a blanket of fog, they cut the man into as many pieces as they could, taking care to cut off his head and split it into two. They collected all the pieces and burned them in a pyre, and the monastery was filled with the smell of roses and of wet earth that the stranger's body gave off as flames consumed its bone and flesh.

The young friar watched from the sidelines, and he wept, openly this time.

Years later, the friar used his life's savings to buy a few sheets of vellum from a traveling salesman who claimed to have traveled from Ireland. This vellum could never be traced to this monastery, and it pleased the young friar. That night he began to write the story of the green-eyed man under candle light, and he wrote until the story was told. When he remembered the stranger bound beneath him, sipping water, and the warmth of his loins pressed under the friar's body, he shed tears of joy. He touched himself as he recalled these memories, and he wondered what happened in the heavens when souls left the earth in a violent manner.

CHAPTER 10
THE SKINSUIT

I met Nathan almost a year ago, and though he doesn't live here in Kansas City, he is close to my heart, and near all my thoughts, as always.

Nathan was the person who first locked a collar around my neck and showed me what it means to serve a master.

Nathan was the man who showed me what it means to serve under a disciplinarian, and what it means to relinquish control of my ass, my cock, and needs to him.

Nathan showed me how to sit still while he bound me in rubber sacks, waiting for his next move.

Nathan lived far away from me, and though he'd visited Kansas City often, we had always come together in his hotel rooms.

Winter was here. I had packed most of my things and given away the rest to charity. I was ready to disappear.

Except this time, I wanted Nathan to meet me on my turf, in my home, one last time. He had never fucked me in the place where I lived.

I had grown accustomed to my new body a little more. For the time being, I had stopped changing, but the current state I was in was drastic. I stood at 6'3", and my body's contours created a symmetry of legs, back, chest, and arms, packed with the muscle of a weightlifter and lean like that of a bodybuilder. Despite my size, I was limber and agile. I was starting to control my own new flesh, and I felt lithe.

All my hair was now raven-black, glossy, and thick, covering my legs, ass, and chest, delineating every muscle. My former blond whiskers were now a thick black beard, which I shaved clean each day as a reminder that I was still human. I had never dreamed in the wildest and most secret of my young dreams that I would ever have enough hair for a beard. And now, there it was, a mask of hair, but a mask I liked nonetheless.

Sometimes the face in the mirror looked feral to me.

Sometimes the gigantic proportions of my body frightened me.

And my urges, the secret urges that I couldn't tell Nathan about, they swelled inside me, like steam in a pressure cooker.

Nathan had given me a set of rules and I followed them.

There is only service to Master Nathan. There are the responses of yes, sir and no, sir.

There are no outside relations in this relationship. There is only one person that can have my body, and that is Master Nathan.

I must never tell anybody about the secrets of my transformation or about the superhuman strength I feel.

These rules got me hard, very hard. But they didn't help me understand what was happening to me. Nathan's advice to keep quiet was sound, but when I asked about what he thought was happening, he simply said it was better to avoid attention. This was something I could live with, he said.

Nathan didn't know about other powers I had discovered recently, and I wanted to share them with him, but it was difficult when most of our sessions started with a struggle to gag me into silence. Sometimes it was a ball gag, sometimes it was a muzzle. Nathan also liked to use his dirty socks and underwear, and he would jam them deep in my mouth, finishing it off with several layers of duct tape.

During our deepest and best bondage sessions, I would float away into a silent place in my submissive state, and I would hover there, like a yogi in the midst of a meditation practice, and ponder my questions. I had started changing into this dark-haired muscle beast soon after I met Nathan, but now I was sure that he was not the one who had triggered it. As I lay bound in a hog-tie, hooded with my prick pointing down into the ground, I realized that the inception point of my troubles was the night I got stabbed and ended up in the ER. The knife wounds had nearly killed me, and my heart had shut down. I had seen no tunnels of white light and no voices from God. Instead, I had witnessed burst of golden and white shapes, geometric nightmares, and visions that etched themselves into my retinas. They had filled my chest with heat, and I had come out on the other side, alive, but *triggered*. I had been triggered, and now I stood taller, like a giant. I was 60 pounds heavier and built like Heracles.

All my life I had wanted to break free from my insect-like body, that skinny body, and now my wish had come true.

I was becoming used to this body, but the other powers, the dark powers that showed up unannounced, I didn't want them. I feared them.

I wanted my job back, too. I still wanted to help people, and to combat the diseases that ate away at them.

But to do so, I had to disappear from America for a while, and I needed to say goodbye to my former life. This included saying goodbye to Nathan.

I would explain it to him later, but much later. I planned to do this in six months, by the time I had reached the other side of the planet. But for now, I needed to see him one more time. And this time, he would be visiting me in my home, and I would get a chance to be under his control before I vanished.

◆

I greeted Nathan this time fully dressed in a rubber catsuit that he had purchased for me months ago. He arrived dressed in a three-piece suit, and his face, that square jaw and his emerald eyes, greeted me. He moved in close to my face, and he smiled.

"You followed my orders well, boy," he said. He ran his hands up and down the suit, which he had ordered custom-made, since it was hard to find a size that would fit my muscled body. He inspected my house with his eyes, though he looked bored by the place.

"Yes, sir, thank you sir," I said.

The bedroom was cleared of most furniture except the bed. He tied me to the doorframe with expert skill, and using the lengths of rope stashed away in his suitcase, he placed me in a harness that squeezed my cock and balls and framed my thick back and my massive biceps, containing me, controlling me. He forced me onto my knees and I sucked his cock, looking up at his eyes, and he grabbed me by the hair and pumped harder. My eyes watered at the pressure of the tip of his cock in the back of my throat, but I was a good trained boy; I knew how to take it.

Next, he drank a beer from the fridge and came back to the room while I waited for him on my knees. His three-piece suit was his fetish gear this night, and my cock was hard, so hard under my suit. It ran down my leg, and lay there, waiting to spring free from the black latex.

My head was free, and I was ungagged this time. Nathan pulled out a cigar and snipped off the tip. He lit it, and he puffed on the Cuban. He took his time, and silence filled the room. His dark good looks and his suit and tie made me wild with desire, and the cigar stirred something inside me.

After a half hour, he set the cigar aside, and he unzipped himself. His cock came forth, and it was mere inches from my face. I knew what was to come, but the silence between us was making me feel like anything could happen.

Nathan urinated, and a stream of yellow piss came forth from the tip, marking my face, my hair, and running down my rubber suit with my hands clasped behind my back. His piss was a form of control in liquid state. He was marking me as his, and I was there to receive it. I could feel my dick wanting to cum inside the suit, but I did my best to hold back.

"You look like a bodybuilder now, Roland," Nathan said. "A far cry from a runner's build. I liked you blond, but I like you like this, too."

"Thank you, sir."

Next he moved me to the bed and he tied my hands in front of me while he hooded me in rubber. My breathing slowed down as my airflow got tighter through the pinholes at the nose. Once I was fully encased in the rubber, Nathan straddled me, and he smacked my balls as hard as he could. I wanted him to do it again, but he only did it to get my attention.

"I like submissives who fight back, and the time has come to show daddy what you know," Nathan said. "Let's see you wriggle out of those wrist bindings and wrestle me. And don't hold back, fucker."

He spat on my rubbered face.

Breaking the ropes that tied me would be easy, and since he asked me to give it my all, I did. They snapped off like rubber bands, and I bucked under him, throwing him sideways on the bed. He jumped right back up, and he lunged at me, aiming low, toward my thighs, to knock me off balance. He knew what he was doing. He struck me squarely, and though I was now bigger than him, he managed to topple me. I flew off the bed, and I landed on the floor with a thud.

He wrestled me hard, pinning me to the ground, twisting my arms, performing schoolboy pins, and I gave him a run for his money, too. I put him in a head scissor-lock and I grabbed him by the nuts, almost ripping the fabric of his suit. He kicked his shoes off, and he smacked my ass with one of them.

We wrestled on the ground, and I ripped his jacket and shirt off him. I tried choking him with his own tie, but he punched me down. He knew how to fight, and I was not in full control of my big body. I had never been in a single fight in my life.

He straddled me again, his bulge pressed right against my mouth and nose. Man, I loved this.

Nathan grabbed a package from the back of his trousers, and he uncapped a bottle. It was the bottle of ether, just like the first time he had snared me in his hotel room. I loved chloroform fantasies, but I no longer wanted to play that game. In LA, Nathan had injected me in the neck and knocked me unconscious, and I didn't want to repeat that, either. I knew somewhere in his bags, he had prepared a syringe with amber fluid. Each time we played he injected me, even though I resisted.

Tonight I didn't want to get knocked out. I wanted to be conscious. I wanted to be present in this room.

"No," I said in my rumbling voice.

"Slaves don't get to say no," Nathan said, and he soaked the white handkerchief with the ether. I could smell its fumes with clarity. My sense of smell was so sharp now, it was as clear as hearing music.

"No, Nathan, I mean master, I want things to be different tonight."

"Shut up, boy," Nathan said and slapped my face. The slap made me hard, but I had to focus on being clear.

"No, I thought tonight we could try something different."

"I said, shut up, boy," Nathan said, as he brought up the rag. "You get ten seconds, boy, then you get put out," he said.

"I thought tonight you might let me dominate you. I have been wanting to try it on you, and I think it might turn me on," I said.

He looked at me the way a bully might observe an ant before setting it on fire.

"You're fucking kidding me, right, boy?"He laughed. "You? Top me? Fucking Jesus on the cross."

He laughed for a while, and beads of his sweat hit my rubber hood. I could smell his sweat with clarity, even through the mask.

"I have changed, and I feel I should get a chance to try," I said.

"No, I don't play like that," Nathan said. He brought the rag down onto the pinholes in my mask.

Before the fumes could hit my nostrils, I put my hand on the ground next to me and used it as a lever to turn sideways. Nathan flew off me, and I stood up immediately.

Nathan lunged at me, rag in hand, and he plunged into my chest and belly, where he stopped dead cold. He didn't realize how solid my chest and torso had become, and his head struck the valley between my pecs as if he had rammed himself into a brick wall.

I grabbed the rag from him and tossed it. His struggle under my tits was what I wanted, and suddenly I felt closer to my own power. I pinned his arms behind his back and kissed him through my mask. *That will show you*, I thought. But he kicked at me. And it hurt. He wriggled out of my arms and then he punched me, closed-fist, in the balls. I felt a dull ache, but nothing I couldn't handle.

I shut my eyes and I saw geometric shapes of gold, like fireworks spinning. Something was changing.

I heard the rubber that wrapped my body squeak, and my muscles tensed up. I could feel my tissues expand, and I knew I was changing one more time. One of the dark powers was manifesting itself.

"You like to play extra rough, boy," Nathan said, and he grabbed the edge of my hood with his hand. He was agile, and with the other hand he found the zipper. He ripped the mask off. "Let's get your face free so you can suck master's cock, why don't we?" he said.

Nathan gasped when he saw what lay beneath the mask. I already knew what had happened, but I felt calm as I watched his reaction.

Under the rubber mask, I knew that my own skin suit, that thin layer of material shinier and way more erotic than rubber, had spun onto my head. Under the mask, I was covered by another mask. Though this mask had no pinholes, I could breathe freely, as if through a membrane. I was hard, and I could still feel my shoulders and ass muscles popping as I grew a little more in size.

"What the fuck?" Nathan said. "You have more abilities now. This can't be. How?"

"What do you mean, more abilities?" I said.

He looked frightened but also excited, like a boy under the Christmas tree, shredding colored paper to ribbons to get to the toy train.

He came close to my face and inspected it. "You look so fuckable, so ready for me. I can't wait to tie you down like this. I have an idea," he said.

He dug his hands under the neck of my rubber suit, and he yanked as hard as he could. When it didn't break, he dug in his pockets for his Swiss Army knife. He took the blade and slit the suit open down the front. His erection pressed against his suit trousers as he ripped the rubber suit from me. When he was done, he fell to his knees and lifted up his eyes toward the sky.

"So we have found a superhuman. Jesus H. Christ, it's real. You're real. You *exist*." Nathan said.

CHAPTER 11
BEYOND THE LIMIT

Nathan's hands traveled up and down the surface of my suit. He caressed my calves, and he pressed his hands into the stone-hard muscle of my glutes. He knelt for a moment and kissed each one, and the membrane of my suit let me feel his lips as if my skin were bare. I flexed my hands in front of me, and the blue-gray material reflected glints of light in my bedroom. The fit of the suit contoured to every muscle and every crease of my body.

Nathan came up to a standing position, and he put his arms around me. He tried to cross them over my heart, but my chest and back were far too big for him now. I liked the warmth of his body behind me, and I considered how many experiences Nathan had shared with me over the past year. He had beaten me, tied me, knocked me out, and each time he returned to Kansas City to deliver more discipline, my arousal had grown deeper, bigger. Each time I wanted more pain, more discipline, more of his control.

But who was Nathan, exactly?

He was not my lover. He wasn't my partner. I wasn't even sure if he was a friend. He was the man who tied me down and beat me on a regular basis, with my permission. A fuck-buddy, a sir. These were words that attempted to convey meaning, but I found none of it in them.

Nathan came back around to face me. My face was fully covered in the skinsuit, but I could see through its mask with clarity. He looked up at me, then he kissed me. I felt his lips on mine, and I glanced around the room. My apartment stood empty, and my bags were packed.

It was strange as hell that Nathan hadn't noticed that I was on my way out of here. In fact, he hadn't said a single word about it.

Nathan had never visited my home, and now here it was, an apartment that stood as a ghost of its former self. The former home of a nurse, age 28. I had planned on Nathan fucking me here in this apartment, for the last time before I took a break from my life. Today, things were going to change, and this was my way to say goodbye.

That was the plan, anyway. But when I saw the worry in Nathan's face and his glances out the window, looking for cars in the street, I knew something was wrong.

"I know you just arrived, but I think we should go for a ride," I said. This was my change of plan tonight. Nathan always controlled every situation, every decision, but I had to speak out. I had to take charge of the situation and make it work in my favor.

If you don't do this now, you never will. You have to act.

"Sure, whatever you say," Nathan said, "but you can't go outside dressed like this."

I considered the image of me, walking outside in this skinsuit, and I must admit, it made me hard.

"Why not?" I said.

"The world would never be ready for this," he said. He cupped my balls through the suit, and he ran his thumb over the tip of my cock.

"I don't intend to hide forever," I said. *Just for a few months, until I can find a new city. Until I can figure out how my life came to be upside down.*

Nathan shook his head.

"Have you looked around, Roland?," he said. "This thing that happened to you, it's not normal. Trust me, you can't just walk out the door and expect things to be *normal*. You are not normal."

I shut my eyes and tried recalling the geometric shapes that triggered changes in my body. Their round wheels and angles moved by the millions, rearranging themselves and collapsing into heaps. I had learned that when the shapes moved in the back of my mind, I could will my skinsuit to change.

The hood that covered my face peeled itself back from my face and cranium. It receded further, shrinking down the length of my back and my stomach, like an oil spill in reverse. The membrane pulled itself away from the toes, ankles, and calves, too. In a matter of seconds, a compact brief surrounded my cock, balls, and ass cheeks. I made it stop there. It felt right that way.

"Good boy," Nathan said. I had liked his verbal control and discipline for so long, I began to respond to the word *boy* with pleasure. And I had felt this pleasure for almost a year. As someone's boy. But tonight, something was different. I clenched my teeth. I put on a pair of jeans and a t-shirt. Nathan remained perched by the window, looking out in the street for something. He looked spooked.

"I need some fresh air. Let's go for a drive," I said.

Nathan wrapped his meaty arm around my neck as best he could. He grabbed my cock with his other hand. The move was aggressive. Just like it had always been. He was trying to pin me down.

"I'm gonna tie you down and make you hurt, boy," he said. "When we come back from our drive, I'm gonna punish you so hard, you'll beg for mercy."

This time, my nine-inch cock stayed soft. I was not only stronger and bigger than Nathan, I was losing the arousal that his control used to bring me.

"Maybe not tonight," I said.

He turned me around, and he slapped me across the face hard.

"Shut up, boy," he shouted.

He cocked his arm back for a back-handed slap, and when he swung, I caught his arm in my giant palm.

"Like I said, maybe not tonight, *master*."

The color drained from Nathan's face. And he stared into my eyes. He shook his head and helped me with my backpack. We walked out into the parking lot in silence.

◆

I asked Nathan to drive, and we went from Westport toward highway 50.

"Let's go to Powell Gardens," I said.

Nathan did as I asked. Nighttime was coming soon, and I wanted to spend some time in the gardens before the sun set. I kept my eyes on the rearview mirror as we drove. I saw several cars that tailed us. We were probably being followed, and that no longer surprised me. Ever since I had begun transforming after my near-fatal stabbing a year before, not much could shock me. I made a note of the cars' models and license plates.

Powell Gardens felt like a good place to get away this afternoon. There were places in its 900-acre expanse that felt shielded from the world. I had walked alone there many times, but I didn't mind sharing it with Nathan.

I suppose that if we had something resembling a traditional relationship, you could say that the end of our courtship was in sight. But the truth was, we were far from conventional.

All I know is that my desires to serve as a slave under Nathan had changed. I had never known pleasures like the ones he had shown me. A few times, he kept me quiet with a dirty jock stuffed in my mouth and black tape forming a cocoon around my jaw. He had tied my new muscles with thick ropes, and my dick had been so hard as he spread my legs and fucked me until I came in spurts on the bed. It was during these phases of servitude that I had learned what it meant to be a man.

And yet, I didn't just want what he was giving me anymore. My own desire to control, to dominate, and to use my new body to bring these pleasures to another man were impossible to ignore. Nathan did not permit me to have sex with men outside what he called our relationship. As long as this was the case, my own nature would remain inert.

In secret, I had sought out sex with men, and I had violated Nathan's rules. I couldn't go on any longer pretending like those urges were going to go away. It was time to come clean.

I had tried asking Nathan for changes to our bondage sessions. I had imagined Nathan would want me to return the favor of dominance, but he had made it clear he didn't. And now, I knew something had to change.

The gardens were only open for another 30 minutes, and we hurried inside. I walked much too fast for Nathan, whose stride was much shorter. I slowed down for him. I went straight for my favorite spot, Moore Meadow. Here, we walked into a flat field of grass nestled in a dense patch of trees. Magnolia trees provided us with shade and quiet.

"This is my favorite spot," I said. "In a way, I'm saying goodbye to it today."

Nathan checked his watch, and tapped his feet. "Where are you going? Are you going on vacation?"

"Don't know yet. I have to talk to people, I guess. They will tell me where I need to go."

"What people?" Nathan said. "Who have you been talking to? You're not going to do something stupid, are you?"

"Other people will know if there's others like me. Well, not just if. More like where."

"There's others like you?" Nathan said.

"I know so, yeah."

Helicopters cut through the silence and flew in circular patterns a couple of miles away. I no longer felt like this was a sanctuary. In fact, I got the uneasy feeling that someone was watching us. I remembered the cars trailing us on the highway, and I spat onto the ground.

Fuck it, I thought. *Fuck it all.*

Nathan took a seat, cross-legged, on the grass. He perched his phone on top of his knee.

"Roland," he said, "You've become something above and beyond human. Maybe it's time you considered making a contribution to science or better yet, your country. Your country needs you."

My gut twisted in knots. And I felt rage.

"Contribution?" I said. "For months, you've advised me to stay silent, to keep all of this secret. To refrain from telling anyone at the hospital, to stay invisible."

"The secrecy doesn't have to change, but if you were to let the right agency recruit you, think about how much could be learned about your... condition."

The helicopters hovered closer, and I heard rustling in the trees behind us.

Things were coming to an end, and in that moment, I realized how much and how deeply Nathan had deceived me in all of these months. He was the most handsome man I had ever encountered. This was true the night he blew me when I was a skinny blond kid, and it was true now.

"You *are* that agency, aren't you?" I said. My skinsuit tingled, and I felt it creeping onto my skin, and over my torso, to keep me safe.

An alert popped up on Nathan's screen.

"Motherfucking shit," Nathan mumbled. Then he looked at his smartphone again, and he cocked his head toward the sky, where the helicopters floated. "Shit, shit, shit."

He looked up at me with eyes that pleaded. This was the most vulnerable part of him I had seen. It was the side of his psyche that nuzzled me with dry kisses after our nights of hard bondage. His phone lit up again, and he cupped it in one hand, considering its demand for his attention.

"You were sent to track me," I stated.

"Shit, Roland," Nathan said. "You're a smart guy, and hell, you even work in medicine; you surely couldn't really think you could make such a change and expect nothing to happen, no one to seek you out? I'm sorry. I didn't think you would be this naive."

"I thought you were on my side," I said. "What about everything you taught me? What about your ownership over me?"

"That part was real," he said, and he pulled out a badge from the back of his pocket. I could see the letters FBI stamped across the card. "The Bureau only sent me to observe you, to build a relationship with you, to keep up the surveillance. We spotted an anomaly in our reconnaissance system a year ago, on the night you were stabbed. We were able to triangulate the anomaly to the street where you were attacked. If you hadn't filed a police report, we never would have found you. My job was to befriend you and to monitor you. Our sessions with the rope and with the restraints, our boy-and-sir relationship, that part was all my own. That was *real*."

I had cried tears of joy many times when Nathan had mummified me, encased me in bags of leather and neoprene. I had wept, too, in the relief of the showers we took together afterward, soaping each other in silence. I had never dared cross the limits of my own sexuality, but Nathan had been the one to push me beyond them. That, I suppose, had been real. But all I saw now sitting there in the meadow was a liar.

"This is just like your superhero comics, Roland," Nathan said. "Don't you think you should help your country, help other people?"

"Help by becoming a weapon?" I said. I walked to where he sat. I reached out and grabbed a handful of his shirt, right beneath his collar. I lifted him with ease, and I raised him up in the air. He kicked his legs like a baby.

"This is not a world for superheroes," I shouted. My spit landed on his face. "I will never wear a cape or boots. I will never use this body for anything except fucking, you hear me?"

Nathan cringed under my roar.

"There's no need in this world for superheroes," I said. "What we need are doctors, nurses, teachers. I already have a role to play in helping people out, and even if this freakish body gets in my way, I will help people, motherfucker."

The helicopters closed in further, and as dusk crept in, their headlights went on. Beams of light roved toward where we stood.

"I'm sorry," said Nathan, and he reached out from behind his back in one swift arc. He plunged the syringe from his pocket deep into my neck. I pulled him away from before he could press the plunger. He fell back and came right back up, ferocious like a mountain lion.

"The agency is going to bring you in, no matter what you do, Roland. Don't fight the sedative. You've been such a good boy for so long, letting me inject you, there's no point in resisting. It helps keep you docile. It prevents you from hurting yourself. It also sends out a signature that we can read up in the bureau. We've got you tracked, so just make this easy on yourself. Don't fight, boy."

That amber fluid had been my own downfall, and I had let him use it so many times. I had been so wrong about everything.

Nathan reached into his coat and withdrew a handgun. I was strong, and built thick by my transformer flesh, but I still feared the handgun. I took several steps backward, but there was no cover. Nathan took the safety off and without waiting, fired.

I heard the pop of the bullet firing from the chamber, and at the same time, a large object, solid like an armored car, knocked me to the ground. I hit the grass with my shoulder, and I felt several bones break in my arm and hand.

A gigantic body lay on top of me. His name was Victor.

Above me, Victor blocked out the orange light of the sunset. He wasn't as large as I was, but I remembered how dense his flesh felt. I had once shared a taxi with Victor, and he had put his mouth on my cock, and he had shared some of the secrets of the Golden Man with me. Now, he was back again, his chiseled face in a grin, muscular torso swelled with tension.

He looked naked at first, but as the fading light hit his body, I realized he was covered in a skinsuit like mine. His was shaded in a dark purple and green, highlighting his thick buttocks and lean, v-shaped torso. His bulge was packed tight.

Victor's legs kept me pinned to the ground. Nathan's bullet had struck him in the temple, and a flap of flesh and bone hung in the air. Blood ran down his neck.

"Hi, Roland," Victor said. "Don't be alarmed. Just trust me."

Nathan came in closer, now on his feet, and he fired nine more rounds from the chamber. Holes blew open in Victor's gut and chest. He withstood their impact, but he still bled, like any human being. If the skinsuit provided protection, it was limited. It was permeable to ammunition.

"Roland," Victor said, keeping his voice low and out of reach from Nathan. "Listen to me. You must find a teacher, someone who will help you harness the Process. No one before you ever mastered it without years of training. There are can only be one Golden Man at a time. You are special, though, because you broke that law yourself. You must find a teacher who can show you how to control your power."

"But why can't you teach that to me?" I said. I could see Nathan run toward us from the corner of my vision, but I didn't fear his bullets. I didn't fear him at all. "Let's get the fuck out of here and run."

Victor put his hand on my chest, and I felt heat transfer again through our skinsuits. The symbols that I could make appear in the back of my vision burst forth. Perfect arcs and lines of glowing geometry. Victor's hand felt so good on my body.

"Thank you again, Roland," Victor said. "You made my world feel a little less lonely, even for just a few months."

Nathan fired a new clip and his rounds struck Victor's head many times. Shards of bone and muscle exploded. His eye sank inward as a bullet smashed it. Nathan fired over and over, until Victor's head blew apart and his body fell over. The skinsuit flickered like lightning, until it faded out.

I grunted and moved Victor's heavy body off me. Bits of bone and brain slid down my forearm. I had been wrong about the bullets, and wrong about Victor. He wasn't immortal. And by association, I assumed I wasn't immortal, either.

I spun my skinsuit onto my body, using my thoughts of rage and fear to spread it over my body faster than I ever had before. It wrapped my body all the way through the neck. I walked toward Nathan. Bullets could kill me, but I knew he wouldn't shoot me dead. I still had the syringe in my neck. I yanked it out and tossed it in the bushes.

"I wanted to love you," I said, and I pressed my giant body onto Nathan's. He gasped in fear, and he dropped his handgun. The beams of light from the helicopters fell down onto us, and I knew only had seconds left before they shot tranquilizers, or worse, down at me. I squeezed his neck in my hand, knowing I could end his life right there. His eyes went wide with fear, and tears ran down his face.

I was never going to be a killer. I eased my grip and kissed him on the lips one last time. I smacked him on his back, and he fell onto the ground.

I took that fraction of a second to run into the woods and away from the helicopters. These were my last moments in Kansas City.

I ran fast, my senses alive, and the night swooped down on me.

CHAPTER 12
DIVINE PERVERSION

We had come to play, to waste a day together, Michel and I.

Of course, when we met, we didn't know that's what we would do together. I was not a man who liked detours, but this time was different.

I had met him on the street as I waited for a taxi. He bought a pack of cigarettes from the newsstand. The newspaper headlines blared with news about the megastorm sweeping the eastern United States seaboard, and the sinkholes that had swallowed hundreds of people in Ohio. Forest fires raged in California. Riots swept Egypt, Northern Ireland, and Mexico City. The beginning of the apocalypse, cried out the tabloids.

I had been traveling on my own for weeks, choosing trains over air travel. That morning I had video-called Joel back in Kansas City to explain why I had left. Joel, the owner of Our Lady of the Flowers bookstore back there, had been the only person who had really helped me when I began to turn into what I was today: some sort of new being, powerful yet mortal, with abilities I could just barely understand and control.

Joel had given me the only book I carried in my backpack: *The Golden Man: A Gay Bondage Manual*, by Salvatore Argento. The book's stories built a maze constructed of words and ideas with the ravings of a madman. This volume of puzzles and stories of the apocalypse held some of the knowledge I had needed to survive when my body began to change, and it was my most prized possession. Joel noted my darker, bigger appearance on the video call, but he nodded with approval. "Looks like the book did you good," he said. And that's all he said.

After our call, I walked the streets of the city.

I was used to walking now, miles and miles at a time.

I carried only as much as I needed. I had stopped shaving, and my beard was thick, much too warm for the summer months. I talked very little in this time and made no friends. It was a time of loneliness, and it was loneliness that I craved.

I took a moment to cross the street, jaywalking like I always did back in Kansas City. I was on a street lined with cafes and apartments. I stood next to a newsstand, where a man caught my attention. I stepped out into the intersection for a moment. I felt a little lost, and I wanted the vantage point of the street to look at the street sign.

I saw him in profile, a short specimen no older than 30 years of age. His hair was a matted mess of cornsilk yellow, and his faded brown eyes were set deep in his face. Thin lips, and a body that was built thick, like a bear, loaded with muscle, but soft at the same time. I soon came to learn that one of his eyes was smaller than the other, and an appendix removal had dotted his stomach with a fine layer of scar tissue. He smoked unfiltered cigarettes, and the smoke curled around his thick stubble. His dark blond beard formed a shadow that swept up the line of his jaw.

Up ahead at the intersection of the narrow street, a delivery truck ran a red light. The cars that were headed in my direction slammed their brakes, and they rammed into each other, bending metal and crushing plastic in their wake.

It was a minor altercation, but onlookers swarmed like flies to see what had happened. Some snapped pictures with their phones. I couldn't afford to be photographed. I backed away.

I stepped backward and away from the accident scene, closer to where the newsstand provided some shade from the sun. Though my hearing and vision were sharp, I felt dazed, and I wasn't paying attention as closely as I normally do.

I didn't realize that I was still standing in the street, mere inches from the rushing cars.

I should have heard the roar of the motorbike that was squeezing past the pileup of cars. I should have seen the bike and its driver out of the corner of my eyes. I know I should have, but I didn't.

The motorbike slammed into my legs, and the impact sent energy through my whole body. I suppose under normal circumstances, my leg should have shattered on impact, but it didn't. The bike sent me flying backward, and the small of my back fell right on a fire hydrant, and my body tumbled sideways onto the sidewalk. The driver cursed at me in French and pointed at his wristwatch. He spat at me, and cursed again. Then he took off in the motorbike.

The blond man smoking in the newsstand was the only person who noticed a man of 270 pounds strike the ground, his legs crumpled under him and his face red with sweat.

"Êtes-vous bien?" he said.

I nodded. I knew my limits and the motorbike hadn't even put a scratch on me, but like I had learned, I had to pretend that I was more vulnerable to injury than I let on. I rubbed my knee for effect, and I put my hand on the small of my back.

"Merci," I said to the blond man, who put his arms around my shoulders. His hands felt cool in contrast to the warmth of the summer sun bathing us in its light.

I got up and dusted off my jeans. "My name is Michel," he said. I extended my hand, which eclipsed his in my grip. I did not give him my name.

We walked closer to the accident site to get a better look, and though the fenders of the cars there had crumpled and curled, there seemed to be no major injuries. Paramedics examined the truck driver, and soon, those who were gawking at the scene began to drift off.

Pangs of jealousy ran inside my heart. I had been a nurse for all my adult life, and I could never get that job back. Not with the changes I had been through.

I thanked Michel and asked him to dinner that night. He said yes, because he wanted company, and I did it because I wanted to repay him for his kindness. I had been traveling alone for four weeks, and he was the first person who looked me in the eye without flinching at my appearance.

We never made it to the bistro.

I asked him to come up to my hotel room and wait while I could change into clean clothes, and when I emerged from the bathroom, I expected him to be smoking in the chair by the window. Instead, Michel stood beneath me, shirtless, looking up at me to kiss him. "It's Thursday," he said. "We have a whole weekend ahead."

We rolled on the bed, stripping off our clothes under the cool caress of the air that came in through the windows. We wrestled around with joy and a sense of freedom. I spanked his ass a couple of times, and he tried pinning me with his meaty arms. We laughed, and I rolled over on top of him.

Michel pressed his hips against the base of my cock, and I lay on top of him, dwarfing his thick body. He told me he had worked as a fisherman, a bike messenger, and a bricklayer. His meaty shoulders and the softness of his ass turned me on, and my cock pressed down between his legs. He moaned, reaching behind him to touch the large muscles of my flexed hips.

"I want you to be rough," Michel asked. His face was buried in the white pillow, but I heard him clearly. He asked for this without any shame or self-pity. He asked because that's exactly what he wanted. I turned him sideways for a moment, and he smiled up at me, his lips soft and his neck hard and packed with muscle. "I would have a lot of fun, and you would, too," he said. "If it goes too far, I'll use a special phrase to end the scene. Blue shirt. Yes?"

"Yes," I said, and I kissed him on the lips. His mouth tasted unfamiliar to me, and it was a flavor so good, so unlike anything I have ever tasted before, that I have forgotten it now, like remembering a dream upon waking.

"Blue shirt," I said.

I continued to travel light, but in the bottom compartment of my backpack I still carried a few toys. I pulled out a wrestling singlet, a ball gag, and a roll of tape. "Put the singlet on, Michel." I didn't use the word slave. I preferred the directness of using his name. When I said the phrase, his cock sprang to attention, and he stepped into the red spandex. His thick legs and muscled arms, and the layer of body fat that sheathed his belly, gave his skin a soft look, unlike my own ripped body and its coarse hairs. Michel looked perfect. I pushed the gag into his mouth, and he moaned with pleasure. When I locked the strap in the back, he moaned again. He was beautiful, docile, and connected to me in those precious moments.

He then went down on the floor an all fours, without me needing to order him to order him to do it. He came up to my knees, and he grabbed both of my legs, kissing the dark mat of hair on each one, running his fingers into the grooves of my calf muscles.

I removed the gag so he could worship as he wished.

As he worked over my feet with his bearded lips, I did something quick, something secret. I turned him away, to face the wall. And I told him to wait for a second. I spun on a brief made of the skinsuit, thin and light, but strong.

The skinsuit's metallic blue appearance called Michel's attention, and he nuzzled my bulge, taking his time. He didn't seem surprised at the appearance of my metallic briefs, thought he was turned on by its tight contours.

He kissed the mushroom tip of my cock through the material, and he licked my balls and my shaft. He loved his servitude, and his hands crept up my hamstrings and glutes. He breathed hard simply from licking my briefs.

I picked him up with both of my hands, lifting him up off the ground and into the air by the armpits, never breaking eye contact. I sat him down on a wooden chair. I taped his wrists and his ankles to the frame, and I ran a couple of layers of tape around his chest to strap him into place. His pleading eyes and his raging hard-on begged me for more. He struggled the way superhumans struggled in the pages of the comic books I read as a kid. He bucked in the chair and grunted into his gag, reeling with pleasure. He wanted something more.

I gave him a smack on the side of his pec, and as I yanked up a leg of the singlet to free up his cock, I felt free, breaking the old rules Nathan, my former lover, had set up for me. He had denied me pleasure when he had turned me into his slave, tying me in similar ways to chairs, crosses, and his bed. Those sessions had served his needs, and I had learned what it took to serve a master. But things change.

I gagged Michel again. This second time, he quivered with a deeper pleasure.

I liked giving Michel pleasure, even as I handed out discipline that might make his nipples burn in pain and his balls ache with desire. Every lash and every spanking would take him into consideration, just like I considered his cock in front of me now. I put my mouth on the tip of his shaft, and I ran my lips and tongue around and over the foreskin, using my hand to stroke him as he moaned into his ball gag. I relished the look of his stocky body in that red singlet, squeezed tight and sweating into it. I put my whole mouth on his dick and took it in, working up and down.

My body was much too large even for a kneeling position. I shifted over into a full squat in order to take in his cock in my throat. I easily outweighed him by seventy pounds. My legs spread open as I sat on my haunches, and from his perspective, he could see my gargantuan chest, the chiseled rock and fur of my torso, and my rock-hard thighs, also covered in dark hair like some sort of mythical beast, as I sought out every drop of his semen.

Michel's thin lips curled around the red silicone ball in his mouth, and I realized that though he had set his safe word, blue shirt, there was no way he could call that out now if he was in trouble. But I could still read his reactions, and I could still see him shake his head from side to side if the scene went sideways. He looked into my eyes, and I wondered what exactly it was he saw.

I removed his gag and licked his spit off his chin with my tongue.

I blindfolded him using his own briefs, and I twisted his nipples hard through the red spandex of his suit. He was smiling as I did so, relishing the firing of his nerve cells and the electric pulses they sent throughout his body.

I hadn't had sex in weeks, and I felt my own hard-on strain against the membrane of my skinsuit. A year ago, a violent mugging had triggered golden visions in a vacuum inside my mind, and I had learned that those shapes of light had brought on my transformation and my powers.

I shut my eyes. I projected the geometric shapes that my powers required to activate, and I saw them spin like wheels of fire in the foreground of my vision, like a city made of cogs and levers, and the harmony of lines and shapes.

The visions helped me change my skinsuit, and when I snapped my eyes open again, I was covered in that fine sheath of material, which felt both organic and inorganic at the same time. It encased my body from my neck down to my toes. This afternoon, the sun made it look darker, like a shard of mineral in an underground cave. Its gloss made me hard, and I didn't hood myself this time. I wanted Michel to see my face.

I removed Michel's blindfold, and his shoulders shook while he gasped in the presence of my skinsuit. "Please, let me put my mouth on it, sir, please," he said. I moved closer toward his chair, and I spread my legs open as I sat down on his lap, facing him, so the exposed skin of his legs could come into contact with the suit. As the material of my sheath touched him, it allowed me to communicate with Michel's mind at a level that went above what language could say. My palms inspected the rise of his triceps, and they pressed down in the center of his crotch. This time, when we kissed, he attacked my mouth like a wild man, operating only with his arousal. I pressed my fingers against the underside of the head of his cock, and I massaged it until he squirmed with pleasure.

"You look so hot," he said. "Your body —"

I slapped him again, not to make him hurt, but to bring him to attention. *Look me in the eyes, boy.* I came in close to his face and kissed him on the lips. *Good boy.*

I took the tips of my fingers and found the place between the duct tape and Michel's skin, and one by one, I snapped off his bindings to free him from the chair. No knife or scissors needed. When he was free, he put his palms on my muscled tits and buried his face in them. I pushed him back on the chair without hurting him, and I grabbed him by the waist.

I hoisted him up and tossed him over my shoulders, relishing the feel of his glutes under the palm of my hand. I carried him like a sack of cement, and he felt up my back muscles as I walked across the room.

I placed him on the bed on his back, and I took out a rubber from my backpack. He glanced up at me, forgetting I was still sheathed in my skin suit through the crotch. I willed the suit to open up to expose my cock and balls, and I put the rubber on.

When I entered Michel, he grunted, and his smoker's rasp filled the room. I felt his hips grind under me, and I grabbed each of his legs to spread him open to me, to bring us closer. He breathed hard and bucked under my thrusts, and he suddenly reached out and twisted one of my nipples. Hard. The pain took me off guard for a second, and my face contorted. "Sorry, he said."

I smiled. "Twist all you want, fucker, you earned it," I said. He grabbed the other tit and twisted, while my cock moved deeper into his ass.

I took my time fucking Michel, and we fell into a rhythm, and both of us felt the surge of our climax arriving. He clenched his hole around my cock, and I felt my balls tensing up as I put my fingers in his mouth. He licked with pleasure and joy, and I used my free hand to grab his plump ass and bring it even closer than it already was.

Michel screamed as he came. His load shot upward and onto his chest. I cupped my hand over his mouth to silence the screams for a moment. I didn't care about privacy or keeping the noise down. I just wanted to give him the control he wanted. He grabbed me by the waist and kept me close to him, and I felt a well of fire rise inside me. I came too, and I grunted, pressing my chest downward and collapsing onto Michel, my hips still thrusting and my cum flowing freely into the condom. I kissed him, pulled out, removed the condom, and pumped more cum out of my dick, letting it fall onto Michel's lips and his cheeks. He licked the corners of his mouth to catch a taste, and he smiled and laughed as he came down from the orgasm.

Michel turned sideways in the pillow, and he fell asleep within seconds. While he slept, I willed the skinsuit to recede off my body completely. I didn't have to pretend to go change out of a catsuit in the bathroom, and I felt relief.

The sun was still out when Michel woke up.

"Where are you headed?" he said.

"Australia," I said. "But I'm taking my time. I have a lot of it."

"And what will you see there?"

"It's more like *who* will I see there. I'm looking for a teacher," I said. He smoked his cigarette. In my days as a nurse, I had been repulsed by the very sight of tobacco, but I was different now. I could smell the syrupy notes of the burning leaf, surrounded by the marks of Michel's sweat in the room.

"And what are you learning?" Michel asked.

"You ask good questions," I said.

"What is your name? You never told me what it was," he said.

I had done a lot of stupid things in my life before, but this was not going to be one of them.

"Roland," I said. He had earned my honesty.

"Roland," said Michel.

Sharing my name could put me in severe danger, but a man can't leave the safety of his home village and expect to never have to use the currency and the power of names. I knew I would never see Michel again, and this one afternoon, I felt I had nothing to lose.

"Your body," I said, "is magnificent."

He blushed and shook his head. "It's nothing like yours. Yours is perfect. You look like, what do the Americans call it, you look like a comics? A comics hero."

I smirked. I grabbed his cigarette and took a drag. It was the first time smoking in my life. The smoke tasted different inside my lungs than in my nostrils. Greener, fuller. I exhaled and lay there next to him, staring at the ceiling.

"I get turned on by superheroes," I said. "They are kind of my thing. You got me there."

"You know who you look like? The Fighter. Your latex suit, your big chest, the muscled thighs. You look like The Fighter in the cartoons and the films."

I laughed out loud this time and kissed him on the lips.

"You're a good guy, you know that?" I said.

"So American, your phrase, 'good guy.' They say your country is falling into the ocean. That's what the journalists call it here."

"It's been falling into the water for a long time, but yes, things are bad."

"If you were The Fighter, you would help the people?" I thought I heard him say this in his accent as a statement, but maybe it was a question. Maybe both.

"No, I wouldn't."

"Why?"

"I wouldn't be The Fighter. I am not that kind of person. I suppose I would help in other ways. But I would not be a superhero."

Michel let the moment slip by. Smoke curled up in the ceiling.

"I don't believe you," he said.

"If I were The Fighter, I'd use my powers to fuck hot guys and experience every dimension of sex available to me," I said. "I'd duct-tape hot men to chairs and fuck their holes."

"Soon you would be bored, though. The superhero has to help people." Acne scars dotted Michel's temples and his smaller eye took me in with seriousness. I had never met a man so beautiful as he.

"He has to help people." I repeated those words to myself, turning them over and over, as if gazing into a crystal ball.

He has to help people.

Life was not like the comic books. Life was cruel, and as I had learned, science was also cruel, and incomplete. But science was the best thing we had.

Men were cruel, too. Especially the men we fall in love with. I was going to explain all of these ideas to Michel, but I changed my mind and stayed silent.

"I am going to buy a suit like yours in a sex shop," Michel said. "It was very hot."

I let his statement linger.

Michel's curiosity aroused me, but there wasn't a lot of time to talk. As usual, I felt like someone was following me, and to invest time in Michel could mean putting him in a certain kind of danger.

"If I came back to France, how would I find you, Michel?" I said.

"You wouldn't," he said. "I travel, just like you. I will go to Belgium and stay for some time. Maybe visit Cordoba, Madrid. You and I are similar that way," he said. "We travel."

I was much too large for the bed: my back was hanging off the precipice of the mattress, and my feet dangled off the edge. Michel grabbed me close and anchored me, breathing right into my chest.

"The end of the world is coming," I said. I am not sure if I phrased it as a question or a statement.

"Well, we must get more cigarettes and beer later," Michel said. "We must have a party for the end of the world."

My perception of time, as I lay there naked with Michel in the bed, was slow. Dust motes drifted in the room, markers of time, like feathery metronomes.

We lay in the bed, and our hard-ons softened. Our sweat evaporated.

I decided I would wait until Michel and I drifted into post-coital sleep, and I would sneak out of the room and disappear. I shut my eyes to suggest it was time to sleep. In the dark, I saw no spectral shapes, no glowing cities of geometry.

I fell asleep.

A veil of dark sleep shrouded me. I slept, but no dreams arrived.

I awoke, just a short time later, and the orange glow of the streetlamps lit up my skin. I had fallen asleep. I looked at the clock. Just thirty minutes had passed, but I felt like I had slept for a week. The bed lay empty next to me.

Michel was gone, and I was alone in the room. He left no note and no other trace.

I still had much more to learn about how to master the skill of disappearing.

There was a man on the other side of the world, a man of science, who I knew could help me. The newspapers called him the Einstein of gene manipulation. Academics had called him the most dangerous man in the field since Charles Darwin. Dr. David Dallion was his name. It was possible he could teach me insights into the changes that were underway in my mind and in my body.

His research was controversial, and as I thought about crossing country borders for the next few months, I considered how many times I could get caught at immigration, if the FBI were to alert them to the presence of a 6'3" man with black hair and a muscled physique. If I wasn't careful, it was possible an FBI agent who had once used the alias Nathan could be there at the gate, waiting for me with handcuffs, or a tranquilizer gun, or worse. I wasn't sure I was ready to see his face again, but I knew I would never find a teacher, or the nature of my being, by sitting still in Kansas City. I had to move, and moving came with many risks.

Those were risks I had to take.

I packed my bags that night and checked out of my hotel. I wasn't tired, and I knew there was a train I could catch before midnight. I stepped out onto the street and left the hotel behind. I bought a pack of cigarettes so I could smoke while I walked toward the east.

THE GOLD APOCALYPSE CONTINUES

How to Kill a Superhero: A Gay Bondage Manual is the first book in the Gold Apocalypse series, which follows the adventures of Roland in his quest to harness the powers of the Golden Man. The next two books will be released in Spring and Fall of 2014 from Beast Within Books. For more details, as well as a look at exclusive excerpts and bonus material, please visit:

www.howtokillasuperhero.net

ABOUT THE AUTHOR

Pablo Greene was born in Buenos Aires, Argentina, where he studied philosophy. He resides in New Orleans, Louisiana. You can follow him on Twitter at @pablogreene.

Made in the USA
San Bernardino, CA
28 December 2013